PENGUIN BOOKS

A MONTH IN THE COUNTRY

J. L. Carr is a Kettering publisher of standard poets, idiosyncratic maps and unlikely dictionaries. He is also the author of several novels including *A Day in Summer* (1964), *A Season in Sinji* (1967), *The Harpole Report* (1972), *How Steeple Sinderby Wanderers Won the FA Cup* (1975). *A Month in the Country* won the *Guardian* Fiction Prize for 1980 and was nominated for the 1980 Booker Prize. His latest book, *The Battle of Pollocks Crossing* (Penguin, 1986), was shortlisted for the 1985 Booker Prize.

J. L. CARR

A Month in the Country

Penguin Books
in association with The Harvester Press

Penguin Books Ltd, Harmondsworth, Middlesex, England
Viking Penguin Inc., 40 West 23rd Street, New York, New York 10010, U.S.A.
Penguin Books Australia Ltd, Ringwood, Victoria, Australia
Penguin Books Canada Ltd, 2801 John Street, Markham, Ontario, Canada L3R 1B4
Penguin Books (N.Z.) Ltd, 182–190 Wairau Road, Auckland 10, New Zealand

First published by The Harvester Press Ltd 1980
Published by Penguin Books in association with The Harvester Press 1980
Reprinted 1980, 1981, 1982, 1983 (twice), 1985 (twice), 1986, 1987 (twice)

Made and printed in Great Britain by
Richard Clay Ltd, Bungay, Suffolk

For Kathie

A novel – a small tale, generally of love

Dr Johnson's *Dictionary*

Now for a breath I tarry,
Nor yet disperse apart –
Take my hand quick and tell me,
What have you in your heart?

A.E. Housman

When the train stopped I stumbled out, nudging and kicking the kitbag before me. Back down the platform someone was calling despairingly, 'Oxgodby . . . Oxgodby.' No-one offered a hand, so I climbed back into the compartment, stumbling over ankles and feet to get at the fish-bass (on the rack) and my folding camp-bed (under the seat). If this was a fair sample of northerners, then this was enemy country so I wasn't too careful where I put my boots. I heard one chap draw in his breath and another grunt: neither spoke.

Then the guard whistled, the train jerked forward a couple of paces – and stopped. This was enough to goad the old man in the nearside corner to half-lower his window. "Thoo's ga-ing ti git rare an' soaaked reet doon ti thi skin, maister," he said and shut the window in my face. Then the engine blew up a splendid plume of steam and shuffled off, a row of faces staring woodenly at me. And I was alone on the platform, arranging my pack, taking a last look at a map, pushing it into my topcoat pocket, levering it out again to spill my ticket on the stationmaster's boots, wishing I'd sewn on two missing buttons, hoping that it would stop raining until I had a roof over my head.

A youngish girl, her face flattened against a window-pane, stared at me from the stationmaster's house. It must have been my coat which interested her; it was pre-War, about 1907 I should imagine, wonderful material, the real stuff, thick herringbone tweed. It reached down to my ankles; its original owner must have been a well-to-do giant.

I saw that I was going to get very wet; my soles were letting in water already. The stationmaster stepped back into his lamp-room and said something, but I didn't follow his dialect. He seemed to understand this. "I said that you could borrow my umbrella," he repeated in tolerable English.

"Where I'm going isn't too far," I said. ". . . According to the map, that is."

The folk up there have an invincible curiosity. "Where would that be?" he asked.

"The church," I said. "I expect I can dry out when I get there."

"Come on in and have your tea first," he countered.

"I've arranged to meet the Vicar," I said.

"Oh," he said, "I'm Chapel. All the same, if you want for ought, send me word. I say, I hope it's there."

He seemed to know why I'd come.

Then I set off half-heartedly, as best I could sheltering my spare clothes (which were in the straw fish-bass) under my coat. The lane was where the map had said it ought to be. And there was the single building; it turned out to be a dilapidated farmhouse, its bit of front garden sulking behind a rusting cast-iron fence. A dog, an Airedale, dragged on its chain, howled half-heartedly and ran for shelter again. After that, there was a couple of hen-huts collapsing amongst nettles in the decaying orchard. The rain made a channel from my trilby down my neck and one handle of the fish-bass gave way. Then I turned the corner of a high hedge and was in an open pasture. And there was the church.

It was an off-the-peg job. Evidently there had been no medieval wool boom in these parts. This had been starveling country, every stone an extortion. The short chancel had an unusually shallow pitched roof; it must have been added a good hundred years after the main building (which had a steep pitch flattening into aisles). The tower was squat. Don't get the wrong impression; all in all, it was pleasant-enough looking and, when I came closer, I saw that the masonry had been fettled up very nicely – limestone ashlar not rubble. Even between the buttresses it had been beautifully cut with only a hint of mortar and, near-enough drowning as I was, I silently applauded the masons. The stone itself – just a tinge of pale yellow in it, magnesium – it must have been quarried near Tadcaster and ferried up the rivers. Don't let the detail irritate you: even in those far-off days I thought rather highly of myself as a stone-fancier.

The graveyard wall was in good repair, although, surprisingly, the narrow gate's sneck was smashed and it was held-to by a loop of binder twine. There were some good eighteenth-century headstones, their lichen-stained cherubs, hour-glasses and death's heads almost hidden by rank grass, nettle patches and fool's parsley. I glimpsed two or three spikes of a family grave overwhelmed by briars: a grey cat peered out, glared hostilely at me and was gone. Heaven knows what else was living there: nowadays, it would have been a listed wildlife sanctuary.

The rain-gutters and down-pipes – I couldn't help myself: I had to see if they were coping. So I threshed around the building. Not a gusher anywhere, not a trace of wash on the walls! Damp's the doom of wall-paintings. If there'd been even one green wall, I might as well have turned around there and then and let myself be washed back to the station.

So I came back to the little porch, its stone sitting-slabs polished by five hundred years rubbing from backsides of funeral parties faint from incense or remorse.

I twisted the ring handle and pushed the door open. It squealed – a warning I was to be grateful for during the next few weeks. And there I was. By and large, it was what I'd guessed it might be – a stone-slabbed floor, three squat pillars on each side of the nave, two low aisles and, beyond, a chancel (as much as I could see of it) strenuously re-organized by some Tractarian incumbent. The roof was a good sound job; it might have been a ship's bottom wrong way up. And it looked as though there'd be some interesting bosses. But, of course, it's the smell of places, always the smell, which makes the immediate impression – and this smell was damp hassocks.

The scaffolding, as I'd been told by letter, was rigged up, filling the chancel's arch. There even was a ladder roped to it and this I immediately climbed. Much can be said against the Revd. J.G. Keach. Alas, yes. But, when he stands before the Judgement Seat, this also must be said in extenuation – He was businesslike, Lord. And, in Englishmen, this is a rare virtue. We could have done with a few depot supply-majors like him in France. He had said that the scaffold would be ready and it was. He had said that, if I arrived on the quarter-past seven train, he would meet me in the church at seven-thirty. And he did.

And that was how I first saw him, his precise businesslike letters made flesh, standing in the doorway below me, seeing by wet footprints that I had come. Like a tracker-dog he looked along their trail to the foot of the ladder and then up it.

"Good evening, Mr Birkin," he said, and I climbed down. He was four or five years older than me, maybe thirty, a tall but not a strong-looking man, neatly turned-out, pale-eyed, a cold, cooped-up look about him and, long after he must have become used to my face-twitch, he still talked to someone behind my left shoulder.

He went straight to business. "About your living in the bell-chamber. I am by no means terribly enthusiastic; well, put it this way, the idea doesn't appeal to me. Surely I made it quite clear in our correspondence that Mossop must ring the bell each Sunday and that the rope passes through a hole in the floor. I hoped that you would make other arrangements – lodgings or a room at the Shepherds' Arms."

I muttered something about money.

"The stove," I said. "What about the stove? You didn't say one way or the other. Can I use it? The rain . . . like today. . . ." My stammer put him off for a moment or two.

"It wasn't in the contract," he hedged, somehow managing to imply that neither were my stammer and face twitch. "There was no mention of the stove initially. We have to think about *our* expenses, too, you know. You stated that you would be bringing a primus stove. In your first letter. This one." He took it from a pocket and pushed it at me. "Halfway down the second page."

"I might set something afire," I countered, feeling rather pleased with myself; people don't realise that a stammerer has more time to deal with awkward questions, and I chased this up with, "And don't forget the Insurance. It's what they term, Using a building for Unnatural Activities. Meths and paraffin . . . ancient timber . . . tinder-dry . . . sure-fire reason for putting up the premium. I had an uncle who was an insurance-collector. . . ."

Unnatural Activities told on him. Unnatural Activities are bad enough in London but what they got up to in the country – and up here in the North on top of that! And it's well known that Sin is blown up twice life-size when reporting to the clergy.

"Oh, alright," he said irritably. "I suppose you can use it if you say you must." Then, like all people who give in too easily, he began to grub up a few restrictive clauses to recover face. "But you must see that it's left in an Acceptable State on Sundays, and, naturally at all times, you will remember that this is a Consecrated Place? You *are* a Churchman?"

Oh yes, I told him, he could rely on me. I saw him considering a possible ambiguity here, wondering what exactly he could rely on me for. From his expression – the worst. I didn't look like a Churchman. Indeed I looked like an Unsuitable Person likely to indulge in Unnatural Activities who, against his advice, had been unnecessarily hired to uncover a wall-painting he didn't want to see, and the sooner I got it done and buzzed off back to sin-stricken London the better.

"It's very unusual," I said.

"Oh?"

"This stove," I said. "It's unusual."

"Hopelessly out of date," he said. "I'm going to have it out before winter. I have a catalogue which illustrates a newly patented device with a twin boiler. Each boiler is enclosed in a water-jacket, thus ensuring a steady dependable outflow of heat. And it is guaranteed noiseless."

He sounded a different man glibly boasting about that stove, even though it was no nearer Oxgodby than a catalogue's page.

"This one either is excessively hot, on occasions, red-hot (in point of fact) or else just keeping itself and no-one else warm." And he gave it a resentful little kick. They glowered at one another like ancient enemies.

He may well have said much more but I didn't hear him because I was examining the stove with great attention. Some mechanical things fascinate me. Until that day, chiefly clocks or anything run by clockwork. I'd not considered the possibilities of coke stoves. There seemed to be several knobs and toggles for which I could see no purpose: plainly, this damned big monster was going to provide me with several pleasurably instructive hours learning its foibles, and I hoped that he wouldn't manage to get it out until after I'd gone. Anyway, I gave the place he'd unfairly struck a propitiatory rub. Properly coaxed along and with the sympathetic cooperation of Mossop (whoever he might be), it might have been employed with devastating effect to drive home a sermon on Hell-fire and the Bottomless Pit.

It had a largish oval escutcheon wreathed in cast-iron roses announcing that BANKDAM-CROWTHER LTD. of Green Lane, Walsall had manufactured it under Patent 7564B. Well now, that *was* a pedigree to conjure with! More than a pedigree – a dynasty . . . Bankdam-Crowther, the Hapsburgs of the stove world! God knows what had happened to Bankdam, but I recalled reading in the *Daily Mail* that Crowther had cut his throat before jumping from Bridlington Pier to make an absolutely dead-sure end. Nothing at all to do with his stoves: it was women and horses he didn't understand. So they didn't make them anymore. Shocking loss to those parts of the world that need warming by coke. In fact, the last one I'd seen was at Ypres. After a direct shell burst, the church had collapsed in on itself. But not the good old

Bankdam-Crowther! Marvellous tribute to the British workman!

The rain rattled on the roof. "What is it you actually object to?" I asked.

"It rumbles," he said impatiently, ". . . and disturbs the prayers and hymns: empty-headed children seem to find it funny. And then there is the blow-back and, when this . . . well, blows back, it erupts. Smoke, sparks, ash . . . yes, ash, it showers ash on the congregation. I have had several complaints. During evensong on January 15th this year, some even fell on the choir during the anthem. Not merely ash! Ashes! I've had an expert from York to look at it. He charged us a guinea and said it wouldn't give us any more trouble. But within the month it was at it again. Just now it seems to have settled down; I know you can be relied on not to interfere with it."

Plainly he knew that he couldn't rely on me at all. I looked thoroughly unreliable; my topcoat betrayed me. There was my face, the left side, too. Like his Bankdam-Crowther it worked spasmodically. People like the Revd. J.G. Keach brought it on badly. It began at my left eyebrow and worked down to my mouth. I'd caught it at Passchaendaele and wasn't the only one either. The medics said it might work off given time. Vinny going off hadn't helped it.

No, I told him, he could rely on me and put on what I believed to be a reliable look. As one side of my face was being jerked in another and unreliable direction, I must have looked frightening because he gave the stove another kick – an embarrassed one.

"Now," he said ". . . to touch on a delicate topic." It apparently was going to be very delicate, because he lowered his voice. "Should you . . . when you feel a call-of-nature you can use the hut in the north-east corner of the burial yard. You'll find it quite private – behind some lilac bushes. When last I looked there were a few tools Mossop uses, but there's room enough. Kindly sprinkle a little Keating's once a week and shovel down some earth: it controls the flies."

This must have been a very great effort for him, and there was an interval whilst he gathered reserves of goodwill for a further concession. "The scythe," he said.

"The scythe?"

"Mossop's scythe hangs from a nail there. It is rusting. The nail."

"Ah."

"Perhaps you should ensure that it is safely secured before. . . ."

I thanked him, speculating if it was loss of life or only manhood he was concerned about.

"I told Moon he might use it too. What period do you suppose it to be?"

He couldn't possibly have meant the earth-closet, so I supposed he meant the stove and said, "Oh, about 1890 . . . 1900 . . . somewhere about that time" and wondered who Moon, my secret sharer, was.

"No, no," he exclaimed irritably. "The mural . . . the wall-painting. . . ."

I told him that I couldn't possibly know that until I'd uncovered part of it. The costume would tell me within ten or twenty years; dress fashion didn't change all that quickly even for the well-to-do and, as for the poor, theirs scarcely altered at all, so I was hoping that there'd be one or two rich women. I said that kirtles went out and snoods came in about 1340. But, if he wanted me to guess – and guess was all it would be – I'd say fourteenth century, after the Black Death, when surviving magnates were swallowing dead neighbours' estates at disaster prices and while fear for their own skins was still sweating out some of their profits.

He began to say something quite irrelevant – perhaps that was one reason why it was hard to keep listening to him. But there was a quality in his voice too which sapped the spirit and possibly there was a great deal that I missed (I may have been brooding on Moon and Mossop's Damoclean scythe).

"When will you start?"

I picked up *that*. Well, here I was: I'd started. Surely, that was plain enough. Then I heard him say, "We shan't entertain any Extras."

"There won't be any."

"There *mustn't* be any. You agreed to 25 guineas. £12.10s. to be paid half-way and £13.15s. when Finished and Approved by the Executors. I have your letter here."

"Why just the Executors?" I asked. "Why not you too?" That was a shrewd thrust.

"Merely Miss Hebron's omission in the form of bequest," he lied bitterly. "An oversight, of course,"

Of course, I thought. Naturally!

But he struck back. "However, for all intent and purpose, I represent the executors. I shan't mind if you touch it up . . . any faint areas or even bits which may have disappeared . . . you can fill them in. So long as it's appropriate and tones in with the rest. I leave it to you" (he added doubtfully).

Incredible! I thought. Why are so many parsons like this? Must one excuse their defective sensibility towards their fellows because they are engrossed with God? And what about their wives? Can they possibly be like this at home?

"Of course, it isn't absolutely sure anything's there," I said, trying to sound matey.

"Of course there's something there. I may have a certain reservation (which I'm not prepared to discuss) about Miss Hebron but she was no fool. She went up a ladder and scraped a patch until she found something."

Good God, this was appalling! Scraped a patch! "How big a patch?" I moaned, sounding hysterical and staring wildly into the gloom above my chancel arch – (my cheek-bone clicking away like mad).

"One head, I believe," he said. "Certainly not more than two."

A head! Perhaps *two* heads! Probably half a dozen heads! She would have used sandpaper and a pan-brush. I felt like running up the ladder and beating my head on the wall.

"Then she whitewashed it over again," he went on, quite oblivious to my distress. "You might as well know here and now your employment has not my support. But, no doubt, you guessed this – reading between the lines of my letters. It would never have reached this stage but for the unreasonable position taken up by her solicitors when I asked their agreement to an alternative use for your twenty-five guineas and their pig-headed refusal to pay out her £1000 bequest to our Fabric Fund until the will's conditions were fulfilled."

I gazed up into darkness. However had she known it was there? But what if there was nothing except what was left of her heads? But if Keach, plainly a notable unbeliever, believed there was, then there must be. It occurred to me that perhaps he'd had a scrub too.

"It will be in full view of the people," he complained.

"It?" I asked. "It?"

"Whatever it is," he said curtly, looking furiously up the ladder. "It will distract attention from worship."

"Only for a short time," I said. "People tire of colour and shapes which stay in the same place. And they always believe that they've more time than they will have and that, someday, they'll come on a weekday and have a proper look." I should have said 'we' – I'm just the same.

Do you know, I believe that he actually did consider the validity of this argument before rejecting it. Then he went. He hadn't told me who Moon was. Perhaps we should run into one another behind the lilac bushes.

I ran up the ladder again and did a few gentle bounces on the platform; it was commendably firm. Then I contemplated the great sweep of lime-washed wall before me. Yes – 'contemplated' – no other word will serve: it was a solemn moment. It went (the wall, that is) up to the roof timbers and sideways and downwards to the limits of the arch. Like a blind man I ran the flats of both hands along its surface until I found the places she'd distempered again. By nature we are creatures of hope, always ready to be deceived again, caught by the marvel that *might* be wrapped in the grubbiest brown paper parcel.

But I *knew* it was there. And I knew it was a Judgement. It was bound to be a Judgement because they always got the plum spots where parishes couldn't avoid seeing the God-awful things that would happen to them if they didn't fork out their tithes or marry the girls they'd got with child. It would be St Michael weighing souls against Sin, Christ in Majesty refereeing and, down below, the Fire that flameth evermore – a really splendidly showy crowd-scene. Perhaps I'd have done better to have bargained for payment per head.

I was so excited that only darkness stopped me from

making a start. What luck! My first job . . . well, the first job on my own account. Mustn't make a mess of it, I thought. The pay's terrible but, somehow, I'll survive and have something to show future customers. And I willed it to be something good, really splendid, truly astonishing. Like Stoke Orchard or Chalgrove. Something to wring a mention from *The Times* and a detailed account (with pictures) in the *Illustrated London News.*

Then I climbed down the scaffold ladder and up the belfry ladder but, before I lit my oil lamp, I crossed to the window and looked across the darkness to the village's scattered lights glittering through the rain. Well, I thought, this is home for a few weeks; and I don't know a soul and no-one knows me. I might as well be a man from Mars. No. Already this wasn't true. I knew the Revd. J.G. Keach, probably all I needed ever to know about him. And the Stationmaster; hadn't he offered me a meal? Practically Oxgodby's entire Establishment with Mossop and Moon Bros. waiting in the wings. I was Somebody already – in less than a couple of hours. Marvellous!

That night, for the first time during many months, I slept like the dead and, next morning, awoke very early. In fact, I didn't sleep long after daybreak on any of the succeeding Oxgodby days. The work was tiring – I was on my feet most of each day, often eating whilst standing – and then, at night, up there in my loft high above the fields and away from the road, too far for voices to carry, there was nothing to disturb me. Sometimes, awakening momentarily, I heard a vixen howling at the edge of some distant wood or the scream of some small creature set upon in the darkness. For the rest, only the sounds of an ancient building, a tremor on the bell-rope coming down and out through the hole in the floor, a stir in the roof timbers, stone still settling after five hundred years . . .

During my weeks there I had only two bad nights. Once when I dreamed that the tower was crumpling and, once, sliding forward into machine-gun fire and no pit to creep into, slithering on through mud to mutilating death. And then my screams too joined with the night creatures. Well, there was a third sleepless night but that came much later and for a different reason.

So, that first morning, I rolled up my blanket and, avoiding the bell-rope, walked across to the south window and pulled away my coat hitched across to keep out the rain. It was a simple two-light window, unglazed of course, with a simple mullion strong enough to take my weight. The rain had ceased and dew glittered on the graveyard grass, gossamer drifted down air-currents, a pair of blackbirds picked around after insects, a thrush was singing where I could see him in one of the ash trees. And beyond lay the pasture I had crossed on my way from the station (with a bell-tent pitched near a stream) then more fields rising towards a dark rim of hills. And, as it lightened, a vast and magnificent landscape unfolded. I turned away; it was immensely satisfying.

Then I unpacked my foodstore, tea, marge, cocoa, rice, a loaf, thinking that I should need to scrounge a couple of tins with tight lids to keep the stuff airtight. I primed my stove with meths, fried a couple of rashers and made a thick sandwich. It was very pleasant sitting on the boards, leaning against a wall, because through my window I still could see the hills heaving up like the back of some great sea-creature, dark woods washing down its sides into the Vale.

And then, God help me, on my first morning, in the first few minutes of my first morning, I felt that this alien northern countryside was friendly, that I'd turned a corner and that this summer of 1920, which was to smoulder on until the first leaves fell, was to be a propitious season of living, a blessed time.

I told myself that I didn't care how long the job took me – what was left of July, August, September, even October. I was going to be happy, live simply, spend as little as paraffin, bread, vegetables and bit of bully-beef now and then might cost me. I could have managed on a couple of pints of milk a week, but this weather it wouldn't keep so I should have to have three: oatmeal porridge is very sustaining and needs only warming to make a second meal. So I reckoned that, with no rent to pay, I could manage comfortably on fifteen bob a week, maybe even ten or twelve. In fact, the twenty-five quid they'd agreed to pay me might be made to spin out until cold weather drove me back to winter quarters in London.

The marvellous thing was coming into this haven of calm water and, for a season, not having to worry my head with anything but uncovering their wall-painting for them. And, afterwards, perhaps I could make a new start, forget what the War and the rows with Vinny had done to me and begin where I'd left off. This is what I need, I thought – a new start and, afterwards, maybe I won't be a casualty anymore.

Well, we live by hope.

There was a second window in the loft; I'd noticed it the previous evening. It had some sack-cloth tacked across, so I'd supposed that it must cover some sort of opening. Now I pulled it away.

Over the years I suppose that I must have grubbed

around scores, maybe hundreds of churches, but do you know, that tug revealed the most extraordinary sight of all. There, almost scraping my nose, was a baluster, a hulking big Anglo-Saxon baluster. And I began laughing. Although I'd never seen one before, I recognized it immediately from good old Bannister-Fletcher, our bible in Miss Witherpen's English Architecture class. "Draw a baluster" she used to chide. "Go on, never mind fiddling about with fancy Corinthian capitals – draw an English baluster." (I still can.)

And now here was one – a crude tub of stone with a pair of double hoops top and bottom. 'Go on – draw a baluster!' If I'd been Joseph Conrad I'd have gone into a peroration about the lost land of youth. My first real-life baluster! And for a few weeks, to all intents and purpose, I owned it: it was *my* baluster. So I stroked its belly – once for Bannister, once for Fletcher and once for the Workmen of the World long dead, and those, like me, still quick.

I looked down into the nave. The light wasn't good and, on the platform near the roof timbers, far too dark to make a start on the wall. So I went down and had a look round the building. Over-all, because of its low nave arcade and the pair of wide aisles, it was a good-looker; in detail (excepting, of course, my baluster) it was on the dull side. However, there was one good wall monument – a Baroque bas-relief of a well-built young lady, Laetitia Hebron, modestly hiding her essential glory by hanging on tight to a shroud as she clambered from an elegant catafalque. All very nicely carved by one A.H. in 1799 – along with a few rather fine lines by her young husband. Well, anyway, I wanted to suppose that he hadn't found them in a catalogue. Latin, of course, but I got its drift . . .

Conjugam optima amantissima et delectissima
Most loving and delightful wife

and on through eleven lines listing her matchless charms, to the twelfth, a single word, his sad last farewell – *Vale*.

I had a second look at Laetitia, a long look after that testimonial. Her tightened shroud showed her to advantage. And she had a friendly face with a teasing upward turn of her lips, *'Conjugam optima amantissima et delectissima . . .'* Well, he was right. He'd had better luck than me.

Then I carted my kit up the ladder and laid it out – a lancet (for lifting limewash), a jar of alcoholic solution of hydrochloric acid, brushes, dry colours, a jar of distilled water to dilute ammonia . . . most of it handed on to me by Joe Watterson when he announced that he'd done his last job and wished me luck.

'It's a profession, my boy' he had said. 'And a bloody perilous and penurious one but, if a profession's a skilled job that not so many men can tackle, then it's a profession alright.' And he'd laughed sardonically into his beard. 'Why we're near enough extinct; there's only the two of you in it, and George Peckover's eyesight's getting so bad he'll fall off a ladder any day now. Then you'll be able to starve without competition.'

I moved gingerly about my new territory. Just above head level the roof's keel drove back to bed itself into the tower, punctuated at its crossings by three quite extraordinary bosses, their original colour preserved by the gloom which lingers perpetually in the fastnesses of high roofs. It was a splendid medieval gallery – nearest me, an almost Spanish head of the stricken Christ caught amid the leaves of a gallows tree; further along, a golliwog devil thrusting his grinning head between a couple trapped in the wrong bed; finally, a plump woman holding a blue shield of lilies. It proved what every true church-crawler knows – there's always something of surpassing interest in any elderly building if you keep looking.

Then the door squealed and a middle-sized sturdy chap was gazing up at me, appraising, taking in as much as he could. He had a confident-looking round face, blue, knowing eyes. "Good morning," he said. (He had a highish voice of exceptional clearness.) "Good morning! I'm Charles Moon" and he pulled a squashed tweed hat off his tousled fair hair. "I'm digging next door. In the meadow. You may have seen my tent? I'd meant to let you settle in but felt I *had* to come and have a look at you. Well, partly that, but really because I get so stiff in the night my legs get me up, so that I make a point of stumping across most mornings to see if Laetitia's managed to climb out during the night." He waved a hand at the south aisle.

"I'll come down," I said and did. He was twenty-seven or eight, a stiff shortish man who stood as though he'd taken root. And his "All thy waves and billows have gone over me" look gave him away earlier even than the three holes in the tunic's shoulders where his captain's pips had been.

I liked him from that first encounter: he was his own man. And he liked me (which always helps). God, when I think back all those years! And it's gone. All the excitement and pride of that first job, Oxgodby, Kathy Ellerbeck, Alice Keach, Moon, that season of calm weather – gone as though they'd never been.

We went out into the sunshine and leaned on the wall. I asked him if he would be staying long and he pointed to his tent. "Till the first frosts close me down. I'm reckoning to save enough to get me to Ur this coming winter. Woolley's uncovering the Ziggurat: he'll give me a job when I turn up."

Later, I recognized this as vintage Moon – absurdly ingenuous in his belief that all would be well. "Wooley'll give me a job!" And, of course, he would. One had this fantastic vision of him dropping off the once-daily Basra-Baghdad train at Ur Junction, three huts and no platform, slogging across stones and sand, calling, "Here I am. We've not met before so you don't know me. The name's Charles Moon. What can you find me to do?"

I asked him what he was looking for. He laughed. "Well, officially, for the grave of Miss Hebron's forebear, one Piers Hebron, 1373 plus. She'd come across a reference to his excommunication and decided he must have been put outside the yard. I'm to find him or, at anyrate, look for him. She set aside £50 to fence him in." He hurried through the items as if they didn't interest him.

"No bones, no cash?"

"Lord, no. I'm not a bounty hunter. The contract says I'm to make 'reasonable efforts over a reasonable period'. The executors agree that three or four weeks will satisfy them and not to worry too much if nothing turns up."

"And do you really expect to find it . . . him? I mean he could be anywhere. And didn't families like the Hebrons have the priests in their pockets? He's probably settled in a prime site under the altar."

Moon grinned. Much later, I recalled it was an old-fashioned grin (as they called it in those parts). "Well," he said, "perhaps you're right," and waved vaguely, taking in not only the meadow but the entire parish. "That's exactly what I told the old boy. The old boy? Her brother, the Colonel . . . no, no, Boer War. He saw my point. 'Absolutely damned right, Moon. Just what I told

Addie. Lot of nonsense, Addie, I said. Could be anywhere. Could be those bones Mossop turned up by the cucumber frame. Made no difference. Always came back to the same story – "I suppose I can spend my money how I like, Ted. I'm going to leave you more than you'll ever need." Damned silly woman!' "

Moon sniggered. "I'm mortified that I never met her," he said and fished into a pocket for his wallet. "Look, here's a snapshot of our benefactor: Mossop lent it me. It's a bit faded."

I examined Miss Adelaide Hebron with immense interest; my first employer! She was a long-headed woman, her fair hair combed straight back, a faintly cynical smile turning up one corner of her lips, pale eyes, very fine nose. A colonel, particularly a Boer War colonel, hadn't an earthly against that field-marshal's face.

"I've a feeling I might have hit it off rather well with her," Moon said. "I think she'd understand my not giving a damn whether I do or don't dig the old devil up. Pity she didn't put up the money without waiting to die first: I just might have enjoyed her daily inspection."

"Well, if you feel like that about it – I mean not bothering to do the job, why did you come?" I had to ask: it seemed a bit of a fraud.

"Why, I saw at once what there was here," he replied, as though astonished that I hadn't seen too. "Well, perhaps that's not strictly true. Probably fairer to say I recognized its possibilities. So I didn't clinch the deal till I had an RFC pal fly me over in his old stringbag. All very unofficial. We came over here in the late evening. That's the time of day to see what went on in the year dot. . . .

"I was right; it showed quite distinctly – a basilica. If the Saxons had had such things, it would have been called a chapel. Probably about 600 . . . 650. Very very early, can't have been long after their first sharp attack of Christianity, because it's built in the middle of an earlier cemetery. Not like yours of course – earthenware cremation jars, hundreds of them; the meadow's a pincushion. But not a hope of anyone casually noticing.

"I ought to let Someone Official know about it. And of course I shall. But not until I've plotted the building's foundations and got answers to two or three things that puzzle me. The locals have it fixed in their heads what I'm looking for, so any stones they see are what's left of an old cowshed. I'm only telling you because you're bound to have have tumbled to it anyway, living on top of me as it were."

Well, I wouldn't have had the nerve to have got away with it. Being paid for one job and doing another!

"I've no pricks of conscience about it," he went on, as though guessing my thoughts. "None whatever. It's too early to go off to Ur. I've no people and don't get on with my sister's husband. Well, that's not strictly true; we rub along, but we're not each other's cup of tea. But that's not here nor there. I feel it's Addie's money well spent. Anyway, I wouldn't put it past her not guessing this was no ordinary meadow. Besides, when I've finished the survey, I'll find time to prod around for the old boy's bones. Just for the look of the thing. . . ."

Hindsight, of course, but it came later to me that, even as we stood there talking, he knew exactly where he'd find the grave.

"Well, what are we standing around here for?" he said. "Come over and I'll brew up."

I told him that I'd already eaten breakfast.

"Oh come on," he said. "I don't need to be told you didn't catch that twitch on the North-Eastern Railway, so we may as well start straight away swapping stories about the same bloody awful place. Come over and have a mug. God knows we both must have wondered if we'd ever drink another. And anyway, it's your turn to tell me about *your* job."

So we walked over his magic meadow to the tent. To my astonishment, it was pitched over a pit. "It's better insulated," he said. "And besides, it's like old times: I developed a great affection for holes. You up your ladder, me down my hole . . . we're survivors. Look, this evening, we could have a jar at the Shepherds' Arms and you could meet a few locals."

I didn't say yes and I saw that he guessed money was tight and that Keach hadn't handed over any yet, because he didn't repeat his suggestion. Instead, he patted his left leg and said, "I told you I stiffened up in the night. Well, that's not strictly true: it's shrapnel they didn't dig out."

All this time he was boiling a kettle and, when he'd poured out a couple of mugsfull we wandered back to the churchyard wall. "There – to your left," he said. "See that slight subsidence. No? Never mind, take my word for it, there is one; perhaps you'd see better if the grass was shorter. Roughly, it's about nine by five, which is about right, and part of it's under the wall. Proves that it's been rebuilt . . . several times."

He looked at me. Evidently I wasn't getting the message. "Look," he said, "they weren't like us. Their minds worked differently. Religion was magic. They believed all they were told. If his folks couldn't wangle him into the church or its yard, they'd plant him as near as they could. Even if he'd been a nobody, they'd have done that. And they wouldn't have dropped him in like a dead cat; he would rate a stone coffin which probably will have survived intact."

He stroked his chin and looked speculatively at me. Then he grinned.

"We're two of a kind," he said. "Experts! Damned irritating!" He sat down and leaned his back against the wall.

By this time the sun was well up and someone was crossing the meadow . . . perhaps Keach to check progress. But it wasn't.

"Oh Lord, it's the Colonel," Moon exclaimed. "He wanders around like a lost soul. Look, don't go. Wait a couple of minutes: you might as well because he'll only pursue you up your ladder."

He was a tall drooping man, carelessly dressed, disorganized, remote, the sort of man you couldn't make any contact with, who didn't even *look* as though he was listening. Maybe he was a very shy man who made himself butt in on people and affairs which didn't really interest him. Perhaps his sister, the redoubtable Adela, had been his life-line and now he was adrift.

"Ah!" he said, "Hello! Yes. Making progress, pushing ahead?"

Moon evidently had learnt exactly what response was expected; he said nothing but rearranged his face so that it could have meant anything. I thought his performance admirable. He also stood up and, as far as I recall, he did this for no-one else unless he happened to be standing already.

Anyway, the Colonel stirred around a bit and unknowingly prodded his ancestor's grave-designate with his foot. "Ah!" he said. "Yes. Very interesting. Like having you chaps around. Makes a change. Stay as long as you like. Well, must be getting along. Getting in your way."

"This is Mr Birkin, Colonel," Moon said. "He's come

to put us in the picture about what's above the chancel arch."

The Colonel looked at my boots. "Jolly interesting," he said. "Stay as long as you like, Birkin. Care to umpire for us on Saturdays? Mossop says he can't stand for too long at a time these days. Well, would have liked to have stayed longer. Another morning perhaps. Must be on my way. I'll tell Mossop you'll take over the umpiring. Very civil of you."

He dawdled off. Then he turned. "Found anything out of the ordinary, Moon? Artefacts? No gold bits and pieces I suppose?"

Moon looked more mournful than ever but acknowledged the reasonableness of the enquiry by uttering a strangled sound.

"Mustn't mind my asking. Just showing an interest. Stay as long as you like." And he shambled off.

I never exchanged a word with the Colonel. He has no significance at all in what happened during my stay in Oxgodby. As far as I'm concerned he might just as well have gone round the corner and died. But that goes for most of us, doesn't it? We look blankly at each other. Here I am, here you are. What are we doing here? What do you suppose it's all about? Let's dream on. Yes, that's my Dad and Mum over there on the piano top. My eldest boy is on the mantelpiece. That cushion cover was embroidered by my cousin Sarah only a month before she passed on. I go to work at eight and come home at five-thirty. When I retire they'll give me a clock – with my name engraved on the back. Now you know all about me. Go away: I've forgotten you already.

That was a fairly typical beginning to most days – a mug

of tea in Moon's dug-out, usually not saying much, while he had a pipe. I'd ask him how things were going, who'd looked into his hole; then he'd ask me how things were going up my ladder, who'd wandered across to the church and, now and then, through pipe smoke, he would look speculatively at me. Now who are you? Who have you left behind in the kitchen? What befell you Over There to give you that God-awful twitch? Are you here to try to crawl back into the skin you had before they pushed you through the mincer?

I saw his questions but didn't answer them. Not because I lacked candour but because talking wouldn't help. They'd told me only time would clean me up, and I believed them. Anyway, all that was past and gone and, in those first days at Oxgodby, I was engrossed in my work. It was tremendously exciting: perhaps you can understand if I explain that, to begin with, I wasn't sure what I was uncovering.

Medieval wall-paintings keep to a well-thumbed catalogue. There are the three voluptuaries displayed in jolly dissipation, then racked in hellish torment; there is Christopher wading through fishes and mermaids with the Christ-child on his shoulder; there are those boring female saints stoically enduring wheel, rack and sword-slicing (these fitted conveniently along aisle walls or above the nave arcade). But the great spread of wall between chancel arch and roof timbers almost always got the Big Treatment – a Judgement.

Well, it's reasonable enough. Big casts need big stages and the tall wall around the great arch could be arranged very appropriately with Christ in Majesty at its apex, the falling curves nicely separating the smug souls of the Righteous trooping off-stage north to Paradise from the Damned dropping (normally head-first) into the bonfire.

So I began my labours at Oxgodby by testing this likelihood, using a short ladder to reconnoitre the apex. And it was so. By the end of the second day a very fine head was revealed. Yes, a very fine head indeed, sharp beard, drooped moustache, heavy-lidded eyes outlined black. And no cinnabar on the lips; that was a measure of my painter's calibre: excitingly as cinnabar first comes over, he'd known that, given twenty years, lime would blacken it. And, as the first tinges of garment appeared, that prince of blues, ultramarine ground from lapis lazuli, began to show – that really confirmed his class – he must have fiddled it from a monastic job – no village church could have run to such expense. (And abbeys only took on the top men.) But it was the head, the face, which set a seal on his quality.

For my money, the Italian masters could have learned a thing or two from that head. This was no catalogue Christ, insufferably ethereal. This was a wintry hard-liner. Justice, yes there would be justice. But not mercy. That was writ large on each feature for when, by the week's end, I reached his raised right hand, it had not been made perfect: it still was pierced.

This was the Oxgodby Christ, uncompromising . . . no, more – threatening. "This is my hand. This is what you did to me. And, for this, many shall suffer the torment, for thus it was with me."

Moon saw this at once. "Mmmmm," he murmured, "I wouldn't fancy being in the dock, if he was the beak.

'And he shal com with woundes rede
To deme the quikke and the dede. . .' "

And, lying abed on Sunday mornings, hearing them bleating away downstairs, I could see him up there in the shadows, unseen above their heads, and wondered if he was the honoured guest the Revd. J.G. Keach and Co. were so blithely expecting.

> "Ha! How say you. Did you fede the hongry? Did you give drynke to the thirsty? Did you clothe the naked and nedye, herbowre the houselesse, comfort the seke, visite prisoners?
>
> And what about poor Birkin, did any of you offer him bed and board?"

Yes, you blasted smug Yorkshire lot, what about Tom Birkin – nerves shot to pieces, wife gone, dead broke? Yes, what about me?

But those condemnatory eyes! "And you too, Birkin! Don't think I've forgotten you. Out there in the barrage, taking my name in vain! It's all down on the slate."

But, for me, the exciting thing was more than this. Here I was, face to face with a nameless painter reaching from the dark to show me what he could do, saying to me as clear as any words, "If any part of me survives from time's corruption, let it be this. For this was the sort of man I was."

Kathy Ellerbeck was the first native who came to see what I was up to. She was the girl who had stared from the station-master's house at my coat and me, and she was fourteen years old, in her last term at the village school. She was big for her age, blue-eyed and freckled, a knowing-looking girl. In those days I didn't dislike children; in fact, I got on very well with most of them. And I had really great pleasure from the sort I could talk to tongue-in-cheek, who knew this and enjoyed it too – talk for talk's sake like many kids enjoy ice-cream.

Well, Kathy Ellerbeck was one of that rare breed and, to boot, she had the sense to know a kindred spirit wasn't going to be on hand for ever and that she must catch the fleeting moment e'er it fled. We understood each other perfectly from the moment she flung open the door. "Hello there!" she called. "Mr Birkin, can I come up?"

I came to the platform's edge, looked down and told her that I'd made a rule that no-one must come upstairs whilst I was working. An absolutely right-down-the-line rule and no favourites. Except Mr Moon. We had a reciprocal agreement – I could go down his hole and he could climb my ladder. Did she know Mr Moon? And how did she know my name?

Yes, she knew Mr M. all right; everybody in Oxgodby knew him and, even though I hadn't had any letters yet, that's why everybody knew I was Mr T. Birkin: Mr Moon had spread it around. And I was right; he wouldn't let anyone into his tent nor go down his hole. And what did the 'T' stand for?

"Well, then," I said, "that proves it; it's the Union. So, even if King George came, he'd have to look down on Mr Moon and up to me. Absolutely no exceptions. Except ourselves. We need to consult on technical matters and also check that one isn't working faster than the other. But I'm willing, grateful even, to talk to devotees of the arts so long as they speak up and don't mind me turning my back on them. And never mind what the 'T' stands for – young girls call me 'Mr'."

"I saw you get off the train," she said. "In the rain. My dad's Mr Ellerbeck, the stationmaster. Dad said, 'That chap from Down South, the one who's going to do a cleaning job in the church . . . he's just got here.' I'm Kathy Ellerbeck."

"How did your father recognize me?" I asked. "I wasn't carrying a bill-board."

"Oh, we know most folk who get off the train and those we don't know, well we know whoever meets them. In your case, Mr Mossop warned us you were coming. And you looked like an artist."

"I'm not an artist so how can I look like one?"

"We know artists don't care what they look like and that coat of yours gave the show away. My Dad said I was to look in and enquire how you were getting on. He said you were an opportunity that mightn't come again in a lifetime in a little spot like this – watching an artist at work, I mean."

"Look, how many times have I to tell you I'm not an artist. I'm the labourer who cleans up after artists. And my coat doesn't signify a thing: I wear it because I feel the cold round my ankles like other people feel it round their ears."

I was glad that her parents knew where she was. After all, no-one knew much about me and I guessed what it was like in the country – everthing had to have a sexual overtone, if it wasn't someone else's wife, it was little girls, boys, or, worse still, animals. Though having a ladder between me and visitors must have been a block to their imaginations but, doubtlessly, not an insuperable one.

"My Dad says it must be a miserable job working all day on your own up there, no-one to talk to or nothing."

"Ah," I said enigmatically.

"We have a picture painted on our chapel wall," she said. "Behind the pulpit. Three big arum lilies. It's very beautiful."

"Why?"

"Why what?"

"Why is it lilies? Why just lilies? Why not lilies and roses or just roses? Or roses and daisies?"

"Underneath it there's printed, 'CONSIDER THE LILIES' in old-fashioned lettering. It's a text."

"What an odd text to have on display in a chapel. I shouldn't have thought you chapellers would agree with that.

> 'Consider the lilies how they grow. They toil not neither do they spin.'

Aren't you supposed to be great supporters of nose-to-the-grindstone? Yet here you are, in a public place, recommending malingering."

She considered this and evidently decided it was unanswerable.

"The man who put the transfer on came from York," she said. "He had a book of suitable transfers and we had to pick one. Mam liked the one he had of roses – 'By cool Siloam's shady rill' – it's a hymn. But, in the end, Mr Dowthwaite and Dad decided that, since it was to be in full view of the congregation, it had better be lilies."

"Oh," I said. "And why? Why not roses?"

"Oh I don't know," she exclaimed savagely and changed the conversation. "About you being on your own up there, Dad said I could leave the gramophone under a seat and, whenever I called, I could play you some records. Sacred songs and solos."

"Alright," I said. "It's about time I stopped talking and got on with some work. Play something."

She wound up the spring and a fruity contralto began to rattle off,

> 'Angels ever bright and fair
> Take, O take me to your care. . . .'

It was no trouble at all conjuring up her heaving bosom and starting eyes as she worked up to a final convulsive wail.

"Ah," I shouted over my shoulder when the record had stretched to its end, "very touching! And very suitable! I'm expecting to come across two or three angels up here any day now."

"Yes," she replied. "It was. Would you like it once more or shall I continue on the other side?"

And she did, working her way through 'O for the wings of a dove', 'The Lost Chord' and 'The Holy City'. She was an honest young girl and an intelligent one. The sort who, if ever she roamed far from Oxgodby, in the right place and in the right company, might find Purcell and perhaps Tallis and come at last to Byrd. Nunc dimittis!

She leaned back, her flecked moon-face shining. Plainly, she had set herself to cultivate me and recognized the strength of her position – there I was up a ladder; escape would not be easy.

After that, she used to come on most days, sometimes bringing her younger brother Edgar who had wide, believing eyes and who only spoke on demand – normally a sharp elbow. From their accounts and from judicious pumping, their mother worked out how it was with me and usually sent a bit of whatever was being manufactured in her kitchen – rabbit pie, a couple of currant teacakes, two or three curd tarts. So, over the weeks, a splendid repertory of North Riding dishes was performed *amanti bravura* to an applauding Londoner, dishes Mrs Ellerbeck had helped her mother bake who had helped her mother bake who . . . Sometimes I'd share this bounty with Moon and it was he who suggested that we were eating disposable archaeology.

Anyway, encouraged by this bounty, I began to cherish the hope of lasting out until Christmas if the weather didn't turn too cold or Keach too hostile.

*

It must have been nine or ten days before Mrs Keach (the Vicar's wife) visited. I didn't work to set meal-times and came down the ladder when I was hungry. And, in the middle of those hot August days, I usually cut two rough rounds of loaf and a wedge of Wensleydale and took it outside to eat. On Saturdays and Sundays, I had a bottle of pale ale; weekdays, water.

It was so hot the day she came that the grey cat let me approach almost to within touch before it slipped off Elijah Fletcher's box tomb into the rank grass and then into its bramble patch. It was here, above Elijah, that normally I sat and ate, looking across to Moon's camp, letting summer soak into me – the smell of summer and summer sounds. Already I felt part of it all, not a looker-on like some casual visitor. I should like to have believed that men working out in the fields looked up and, seeing me there, acknowledged that I'd become part of the landscape, "that painter chap, doing a job, earning his keep".

So I nudged back my bum and lay flat on the stone table, covered my eyes with a khaki handkerchief and, doubtlessly groaning gently, dropped off into a deep sleep. When I awoke, she was leaning against the grey limestone wall looking towards me. She was wearing a dusky pink dress.

"Have you been here long?" I asked.

"Maybe ten minutes . . . I'm not sure." She spoke shyly. A wide-brimmed straw hat cast a shadow across her face so that I couldn't tell how old she was. Then, for a few moments, she stood without speaking, her look wandering across the fabric of the church, then turning to follow the haphazard flight of a red admiral until it flattened against a headstone, pinned to its lichen by the sun. I slipped down from the slab but still leaned against it, drowsy, only half-awake.

"Are you comfortable in the bell-loft?" she asked. "Is there anything that you need? Are you sleeping well? I could lend you a travelling rug; we don't use it at this time of year. My husband said you walked here. From the railway station, I mean. You can't have been able to carry much, so I'm supposing that you're sleeping on the floor. Perhaps you guessed that I'm Mrs Keach, the Vicar's wife – Alice Keach."

I told her that I had a sleeping-bag and there was my topcoat if I needed it, and I was using a hassock for a pillow.

The butterfly flew into the air once more. For a moment it seemed that it might settle on the rose in her hat, but it veered off and away into the meadow. The sound of bees foraging from flower to flower seemed to deepen the stillness.

"I'm afraid that you must think us inhospitable," she said. "All of us in our beds and you up there on the floor-boards."

I said that it suited me very well and that it's what I'd bargained for. At the end of each day I was so tired that it didn't need a feather bed to send me to sleep.

I saw Moon's head rising above the grass as he heaved himself into the sunshine and began an elaborate dance, waving his arms upwards and sideways. I'd seen him at it before. He hadn't found anything out of the ordinary; he was just working off cramp.

"All the same I shall bring a rug," she said and left the wall. She walked forward only a few paces but near enough for me to see that she was much younger than Keach, no more than nineteen or twenty, and that she was very lovely. More than just pleasant-looking I mean; she was quite enchanting. Her neck was uncovered to her bosom and, immediately, I was reminded of

Botticelli – not his Venus – the Primavera. It was partly her wonderfully oval face and partly the easy way she stood. I'd seen enough paintings to know beauty when I saw it and, in this out of the way place, here it was before me.

"And when will there be something for us to see?" she asked.

I told her that it would be like a jigsaw – a face, a hand, a shoe, here a bit and there a bit. And then, imperceptibly, it would come together. "At least that's how it ought to happen. But you don't need to be told what might have disappeared in five hundred years. I can't believe someone else hasn't had a go before me and that I'll find patches of bare plaster."

"Oh," she said, "but isn't that the exciting part of it? Not knowing what's round the corner. It must be like opening a parcel at Christmas. Well, I shan't forget the rug and then you'll have to let me see how the jigsaw's fitting together, won't you. You mustn't mind if I haunt you a little . . . Mr Birkin?" And she laughed, an enchantingly gay sound like . . . well, like a bell.

Then she turned away towards the gate and I turned too and went back up onto my platform. And I wondered about Keach and his wife and how the oddest people meet and then live together year after year, look at each other across hundreds of meals, watch each other dress and undress, whisper in the darkness, cry aloud in the marvellous agony of sexual release.

"You had the lovely Alice to see you," Moon said when we met that evening. "I saw her in the yard. You seemed to have a lot to say to each other. Now, didn't you find her a bit of a stunner? Fancy that gem of purest ray serene hidden away in Oxgodby's unfathomable caves! Well, come on, admit it."

"She's a beauty alright," I said. "Quite extraordinary, in fact. Though maybe she doesn't know it."

"Rubbish!" he exclaimed. "Every woman knows it. But Keach catching her! It's an outrage. Almost as big an outrage as society arranging that from the moment he got her to sign on the sanctified line, other men could go as far as that line and no further. It's a devil."

"Perhaps he's all she wants," I said.

"Oh come on!" he said. "You've seen him. Worse, you've heard him. Let's go up to the Shepherd and sink a jar to lost beauty."

Well, perhaps he was right. Frankly, if Keach really was as awful as he seemed, living with him didn't bear thinking about. But mercifully it wasn't Baghdad, so he couldn't drape her in a yashmak and other men could still cast an admiring eye on his doe-eyed bride. And, as we sauntered back down the road, first smelling, then seeing the swathes of hay lying in the dusk, I thought that just looking at Alice Keach was wonder enough, so that I hoped that she would keep her word and call often to see how I was getting on.

I mean to say – the pride of the Uffizi walking abroad in, God help us, Oxgodby!

The work went well. My picture was so well preserved that I became more and more convinced that, even before it was forty or fifty years old, it had been hidden beneath a lime wash. Why? The priest found fault with its iconography? The local magnates took umbrage at some fancied resemblance? A literate churchwarden thought it old-fashioned for a forward-looking parish? Take your choice. Every week that passes, you can bet your life that, somewhere in this land, there's a first-class row bubbling up about what someone wants in and someone else wants out of a village church.

And then, over the centuries, after each fifty years or so of taper and candle smoke, paraffin lamps, the painting had taken on another layer of cover-up. And, of course, in latter days, the good old Bankdam-Crowther had done its bit, doubtlessly, on a single mad morning's fling, throwing up as much muck as a medieval decade. So, once I got the hang of it, the job followed a steady pattern, cleaning down the years to the painting itself. Well, perhaps I'm making it sound too easy. It wasn't – but I got better at it as the days passed.

Really it boiled down to a game of patience. My first move had been to grid the likely area of colour into chalked square feet and then, as you might say, to inch along, only straying from one square to the next to follow a hand or a face. Because, although Joe Watterson had been too canny to put it into as many words, it simply isn't possible to return a five-hundred-year-old wall-painting to its original state. At best, I aimed at approximation, uniformity, something that *looked* right.

And so (jumping ahead for a moment) it went on, day following day up there on the scaffolding, shuffling sideways and backwards, on my knees, up on my haunches and, when I was too idle to use a step-ladder, stretching my toes. It was like a window in a filthy wall which, every day or two, opened a square foot or so wider. You know how it is when a tricky job is going well because you're doing things the way they should be done, when you're working in rhythm and feel a reassuring confidence that everything's unravelling naturally and all will be right in the end. That's about it: I knew what I was doing – it's really what being professional means.

Bringing back that long-dead man's apocalyptic picture into daylight obsessed me. That great pyramid of folk split by the arch! Because it wasn't long before I'd made a foray up, down and across it and had a fair idea of the whole – the judge and his bailiff; below them, the three Lords of Matthew 5, clad first in finery, then only in furnace glare, and, finally, the multitudes trooping smugly right to Paradise or being tossed screaming over the left-hand fiery brim.

Even when I wasn't on the job I found myself dwelling on that immense spread of colour. Particularly during those first two or three weeks when only Moon interrupted me. But then, inevitably, as happens to most of us, first through Saturday umpiring, later Sunday chapel, I was drawn into the changing picture of Oxgodby itself. But, oddly, what happened *outside* was like a dream. It was inside the still church, before its reappearing picture, that was *real*. I drifted across the rest. As I have said – like a dream. For a time.

One day Kathy Ellerbeck brought an invitation to lunch. "Mam says she wants you to come and have your Sunday dinner," she yelled up the ladder. "She says it's our turn for the preacher and it's that Mr Jagger from Northallerton and he's a bit above our heads, but she says the two of you will get on like a house afire. Unless you want to, you needn't stop overlong because, as soon as he's had his dinner, he'll be shunted off into the front room for a doze before his tea-time. But, if you like, you can come with us to Sunday-school – with Edgar and me."

"I'm a bit old, surely," I called back. "For Sunday-school I mean? Not that I couldn't do with some I suppose."

"Well, you could wait outside; there's a seat on the grass verge. Or you can give Mr Dowthwaite a hand: he'd let you look after some of the dafties. Then, if you did that, you could come back and have your tea as well as your dinner and follow on where you and Mr Jagger left off. And that would save you getting your own tea ready, as well as some money. Mam says you're overmuch on your own and traipse around like a man in a dream and need to be got into company. Don't put your coat on unless it's raining."

She was a very organizing girl and had it all cut and dried so, on Sunday, I made an unusual effort to look respectable so as not to let her down, turned up at the bidden hour and, almost immediately, we sat down round the starched tablecloth. Mr Ellerbeck then launched into a grace of impressive length. I found it impossible to believe that, normally, his fellow diners would have permitted him to elaborate in such closely argued detail on the Lord's bountifulness and his own servile gratitude at being singled out as a favoured recipient, so doubtless he was showing his paces to a fellow professional, Mr Jagger.

Often since that long-ago Sunday, I have wondered why it is that men with large moustaches have this facility of declamatory prayer. For the stationmaster plainly had a fine relationship with his Maker (who he addressed as an old and valued friend): he also had a splendid, free-ranging moustache. Whereas Mr Jagger's teatime grace was more propitiatory, uneasily terser: I seem to recall that his moustache was closely clipped.

The Yorkshire puddings, thick ones in onion gravy, were set before us, and Mr Ellerbeck signalled a start by tucking a very large starched napkin into his stiff collar and, this seemingly being the custom of the country, I followed suit. It was an exceedingly hot day and we all sweated freely.

Conversation did not flow easily around the Ellerbeck table. The business to hand was the relishing of victuals and its only accompaniment was some vigorous plate-scraping by Edgar and an occasional suck or half-suppressed belch. The prelude to the main and, as I discovered, the final course was a flashy virtuoso recital by Mr E. on his long knife and steel before carving a very fine joint of sirloin. He carried off his performance with élan and, like any true artist, was not unaware of its effect on a fascinated audience for, cocking an eye, he murmured modestly, "My father was a butcher, Mr Birkin."

But Mr Jagger, too, was no mean performer, quite able to keep pace with our advance across very large platefuls, whilst delivering a lecture on the excellence of the works of Mr Thomas Hardy, most of whose moral tales he claimed to have perused several times. He was so assured and self-appreciatory a talker that really there was no need to do more than demonstrate wakefulness by an occasional nod, so that I was able to look around and take stock of the room's crowded décor.

Basically, this amounted to the square squat table at which we now were seated, our chairs utterly blocking a narrow gangway around which the Ellerbecks edged daily, a standard black-leaded fire-cum-boiler-cum-oven and a varnished dresser. There was a wall clock regulated by a pendulum, a grocer's calendar depicting an elderly lady seated amidst her treasures in a strikingly similar room, and two unusually large pictures elaborately framed, one portraying the besieged garrison at

Lucknow in various attitudes of distress and (unlike the beholder) unaware that succour was just round the corner, and the other demonstrating manifold disasters brought on by drink. Both were crammed with enough detail to provide several years of speculative study.

The room's chiefest glory was an oil-lamp suspended from the middle of the ceiling by four brass chains. Reluctantly, I had to concede that its magnificence ran my Bankdam-Crowther pretty close. It had two knobs and a cut-off designed to immediately extinguish flames if it got to flaring, a beautiful pink cut-glass paraffin reservoir, a standard plain glass lantern and an encircling opaque globe to diffuse a benign glow over the Ellerbeck household. "My Aunt Rose left it to me in her will, Mr Birkin," the stationmaster slipped into an unwonted interval of Mr Jagger's denunciation of Angel Clare's dishonourable dealings with Tess Durbeyfield. "It was her particular wish that I should have it. You couldn't buy its like nowadays: cast-brass, even down to the chains."

I would like to have risen and examined it more closely. Mechanically, it was a much simpler machine than the church stove but, aesthetically, greatly surpassed it. And, observing my quickening interest and not unreasonably considered his other guest had enjoyed a long enough innings, Mr E. went on to invite me to visit his platform lamp-room which lately had received a certificate of Special Commendation from the directors of the North-Eastern Railway when, on their biennial inspection, they had paused at Oxgodby. "On a week-day, of course," he added. "Your visit I mean."

"The District Passenger Manager told Dad he could have eaten his dinner from the lamp-room floor," Kathy said.

This evocation of those grand persons from York, starched napkins stuffed in high collars, feasting (with silver-plated cutlery borrowed from some First Class refreshment room) amongst Mr E.'s lamps and paraffin pleasantly diverted my attention from the hanging heir-loom. And Mr Jagger, taking immediate advantage of our congratulatory reverie, drove a literary wedge between our alliance, hurrying doomladen Tess gallow-wards before he, in turn, was deservedly imprisoned for the afternoon in the front room.

I then went off dutifully to Sunday-school where, as I feared, its Superintendent, Mr Dowthwaite (the village smith) hived off three big lads needing (as he said) 'particular attention'. When he had gone off to his own corner and, finding a study of S. Paul's letter to some near-Eastern city or other kindled no flame in the breasts of my conscripts, I allowed one to teach me how to crimp wheatstraw into buttonholes, whilst another enquired earnestly into the exact nature of the perils he had been warned would beset him if ever he set foot in London. I must have given satisfaction because the blacksmith recruited me for the remaining Sundays of my sojourn.

It was even hotter when we traipsed off down the road towards the railway station. "Let's call and see Emily Clough; she's dying of consumption," Kathy said. "We can give her the cornflowers Edgar's picked for Mam."

Her brother had learnt that both pleas and resistance were vain, so he only looked hopeful that the spectacle of Emily dying would be worth this confiscation. We sauntered on below orchard branches spreading over a hedge until we came to a brick cottage, its front to the dusty road, the other sides looking on to fruit trees and three or four horse-boxes.

The door was wide open and a staircase immediately

before it. "We've come to bring Emily a bunch of flowers Edgar's picked for her, Mrs Clough," Kathy called, and a voice from deeper inside the house bade us go up. "We fancied somebody would call on their way back from chapel. On your way out you can have a jam tart."

"I've brought your star-card, Emily," Kathy said. "Mr Dowthwaite stamped it 'S' for Sick. S's count the same as stars." She ran her fingers along the square. "You only need six more stars for a prize," she said. "Or S's," Edgar added encouragingly.

"I've been thinking what book I'd like," Emily said. "I liked *The Forgotten Garden*. Maybe you'll take word to Mr Dowthwaite to look out for one by the same author when he goes to York to buy the prizes. What are you having?"

"*The Coral Island* and Edgar's having *Children of the New Forest*."

"Isn't it a bit beyond him?" I asked.

"He'll grow to like it later," she replied. "I've heard it's a good story with two girls in it. This is Mr Birkin, Emily. He's the man living in the church."

"I've heard about you," the dying girl said. "I'm longing to see what you're doing and, when I'm better, I hope you'll still be here, Mr Birkin."

An apple tree grew outside her window, its boughs almost pushing into the room. The sun came through the leaves with a soft burnished light. No birds sang in the heat. Summer's heaviness oppressed me. Brother and sister stared at the pale girl: in adults such curiosity would have been indecent. "Who was there today?" she asked. "Tell me who was there."

She listened to the names. Even as late as early spring, she must have gallivanted across ditches and through hedges with some of them. "What hymns did you have?" she demanded. "I like 'You in your small corner and I in mine'," she said. "It's my favourite but it's not suitable for summer. It's a cosy sort of one; it makes me think of winter and dark nights and going to bed with a hot water bottle. I like your straw hat, Kathy. Let me try it on."

The crimson streamers flamed against her pale face. She turned to a mirror and her eyes shone. "I think it suits me," she said. "I like hats. Wearing a hat's part of the fun of Sunday-school."

"When you come next, our Kathy'll let you wear it," Edgar said daringly: no doubt it was an oblique revenge.

Emily did not answer him. Oddly enough, she turned to me and our eyes met. Then we trooped downstairs and had our jam tarts. When we were back on the road and Edgar was picking cornflowers again, Kathy said, "She knows she's dying, doesn't she? You're coming back for your tea, aren't you? Mam said you could."

By this time, I'd got down to my last bob and still Keach showed no sign of forking out a first instalment. It hadn't slipped his mind because he wasn't that sort of man; he was going to make me *ask* for it and this irritated me. But, when I walked up to the village grocer's and found I hadn't a penny to buy a *Daily Mail*, there wasn't much left but to knuckle under.

His vicarage turned out to be in a small wood. Of course it hadn't been built in one: the saplings planted by some earlier incumbent as garden features had become immense spreading trees, and their undergrowth had blotted out any lawns or flower beds that may once have been there. In fact, the drive was now a tunnel and the scuffle of my boots sent wood-pigeons threshing through branches and boughs into the sky. And, round a turn, I came across a hare: it gazed in amazement at me. A jay flew across. A jay! I'd only seen one in books. Why the place was a latter-day Eden!

The house was in a clearing, but what once had been a drive-around for carriages was now blocked by a vast stricken cedar, its torn roots heaving up like a cliff-side and supporting a town-sized garden, its crevices already colonised by wild plants. The once white bricks of the house walls had taken on an unpleasing greenish tinge so that they had a damp look, the windows were mostly shuttered and the building's squarish severity was only ameliorated by a twin-pillared portico. Advancing on this, I found a miniature easel displaying a pallid print of mountains and a lake framed in red plush, the kind of fancy nonsense Victorians posed in fireless grates. As I knocked at the door and then dragged the bell, I considered the significance of this extraordinary decoration and found none.

My several well-mannered tugs were unanswered and, had I not been penniless, I would have gone away. So, quite annoyed by this time, I gave the thing a really savage drag. A good six inches of wire scraped from the hole and, when released, shot back like a catapult. Deep inside the house I heard a bell tinkling. Like distant laughter. As a matter of fact, for a moment, I believed it was someone laughing at me. Perhaps Mrs Keach.

Feeling vaguely guilty, I looked around. Really it was quite oppressive and I marvelled that any practising novel-reader dared put a nose beyond the door at night: an entire tribe of thugs come to retrieve green eyes from little yellow gods stolen by an incumbent's ne'er-do-well brother could have camped there unseen for weeks. As for the vicarage, it could have housed a family of ten with supporting coachman, cooks, maids and all. Where it was plain that Keach could not afford a gardener.

Then the white-painted door opened and Alice Keach looked out. Her eyes were larger and darker than I'd remembered them. When we had met in the churchyard she had been cool, almost too self-contained but, here on home ground, she was overwrought and, before I had time to ask if I might see her husband, she had come out upon the portico and had launched into a rather wild account of what it was like living there, as though she mistook me for a diocesan investigator of clerical dwellings. It occurred to me that perhaps she was one of those shy people who, given notice, can put on a bold front but, caught off-guard, go to pieces.

It was astonishing. Here I was, almost a stranger, being told of a most alarming nightmare she'd been having – how trees had been closing in on her, first swaying menacingly, then dragging up their roots and actually advancing, closing in until mercifully fended off at the last minute by the house walls. And the air, it too had pressed in till she felt the house had become a compression chamber. Actually, she infected me with this obsession – Yes, yes, I told her, I knew exactly what she was talking about, because it was like that when a really big shell explodes; the air in a dug-out is sucked out then blown in, a quite stupefying sensation. I'm sure that she didn't hear me.

Then she pulled herself together. I managed to say that I'd like to have a word with her husband and we set off down a longish stone-flagged corridor, passing by several outsize doors. She opened one of these. The room had two large windows blinded by interior shutters and, but for an unusually small fireplace, was absolutely empty. This plainly was how they'd found it and this was how it would stay until the removal vans came again. As we passed along she touched each door and murmured, "This one too . . . just the same."

Their living room was at the end of this passage and was very long and lofty, with four immense uncurtained windows rising from the floorboards almost to the ceiling. In almost all normal rooms, the first thing to catch the eye is furniture, pictures, mirrors, bits and pieces with significance for their owners. But, in this room, it was bareness. The floor was bare, well not quite bare – there were a few skimpy rugs leaping-distance apart. Three of the walls were bare but the fourth had a single immense piece of furniture like an internal buttress. In any ordinary room it would have been grotesque but, here, it fell into perfect scale. I've no idea what it was. It could have been a Baroque altar-piece, an oriental throne, a gigantic examination exercise performed by a cabinet-maker's apprentice. Perhaps it was none of these things. Perhaps it was only a folly. I would like to have examined it: I mean to say, almost everything has *some* purpose.

"My husband's father bought it at an auction sale. No-one wanted it. He got it just for the removal costs. He just thought it would help fill the room," Mrs Keach said. "We're not sure what it is. Actually, we think part of it's missing."

The room was built for giants and Keach himself had my attention last of all; he was sitting on a hard chair by a rickety music-stand and evidently had been playing the fiddle which now was lying on a small table. Oddly enough, he didn't seem at all put out by his wife's hysterical commentary on their domestic hardship: instead, he listened carefully as though he too was hearing this for the first time, so that it struck me that perhaps they bottled up their trouble until some stranger turned up to have it all poured over him. Actually, I was fascinated because it had never occurred to me that too big a house might have the same appalling drawbacks as too small a one, and only the reflection that I'd no home at all, except the precarious tenancy of a belfry, shielded me from black depression.

Then a most extraordinary thing happened. She stopped talking and both stared in horror at something behind me. Frankly, the hair rose on my neck and I turned with utmost reluctance, really very afraid of what I might see. It was only a cat. But it was the largest cat and certainly the fiercest looking animal that ever I saw in my life. It had a fluttering song-thrush clamped in its bloody jaws and glared through the window, malevolently eyeing each of us in turn. Then it slipped back amongst the rank grass and briars.

This roused Keach to suggest that I might like to see the rest of the house.

There was no staircarpet and even the long first-floor landing was bare boards. "Empty," said the Vicar, doing some door-tapping on his own account. The bathroom was a very large converted bedroom. In one corner stood a smallish painted iron bath with rusty drip-stains below both taps. There was a wash-basin, of course, and a towel-horse, but all these fitments were overwhelmed by a monstrous water-tank, so massive that it was supported not only by cast-iron brackets built into the wall, but by two free-standing painted iron posts. "Mossop comes on Monday evenings," Keach explained. "He pumps up water from a well at the back of the house; a tankful lasts us until Thursday." "If we're very careful," his wife put in. Neither bothered to tell me how they got through the rest of the week.

We trailed along into another large room: it was empty

but for an altar, probably a cabin-trunk covered with a spare bedspread. Before it were two kneeling-hassocks. Next door, there was a little more furniture – a very small desk and a cheap little book-case. On a card-table some washing waited to be ironed, a clothes-horse stood before an empty grate. "Look!" Mrs Keach exclaimed pointing to the window: fig leaves like immense hands pressed against it. "Alice has her fancies," her husband murmured.

That flat iron and the washing made a deep impression on me. In this wilderness of a house, they huddled together for the comfort of each other's company. Neither cares to be left alone in the awful place, I thought. But outside, they're quite different people.

Keach pointed to the ceiling. "Attics!" he said, adding ironically, "And there's a complete suite of cellars too."

We tramped downstairs where I was offered a cup of coffee, but I said that I really must go. Frankly, I was eager to get outside again; that house seemed to gather around one like a shadow. They shouldn't have been made to live in it. And yet both seemed able to throw it off like a cloak. Alice Keach – inside, nervy, obsessive; outside, charming, well within herself. As for her husband, until we met again, I felt quite sorry for him.

She walked out into the clearing with me and paused by a bush of roses rampaging on to the gravel. "Sara van Fleet," she said. It was a pink rose, a single. "It's an old variety. Mind! It has sharp thorns. And it keeps on blooming. You'll see – there'll be some right into autumn." She smiled. "Even if you don't visit us again, you'll know – I usually wear one in my hat . . . Here, take one."

Later in the day, when I had to turn down Moon's suggestion that we go up to the pub, I remembered why

I'd visited the vicarage. But, as a matter of fact, Mossop turned up next day with an envelope containing an instalment – a couple of crumpled pound notes and a receipt for me to sign.

That rose, Sara van Fleet . . . I still have it. Pressed in a book. My Bannister-Fletcher, as a matter of fact. Someday, after a sale, a stranger will find it there and wonder why.

There was so much time that marvellous summer. Day after day, mist rose from the meadow as the sky lightened and hedges, barns and woods took shape until, at last, the long curving back of the hills lifted away from the Plain. It was a sort of stage-magic – "Now you don't see; indeed, there is nothing to see. Now look!" Day after day it was like that and each morning I leaned on the yard gate dragging at my first fag and (I'd like to think) marvelling at this splendid backcloth. But it can't have been so; I'm not the marvelling kind. Or was I then? But one thing is sure – I had a feeling of immense content and, if I thought at all, it was that I'd like this to go on and on, no-one going, no-one coming, autumn and winter always loitering around the corner, summer's ripeness lasting for ever, nothing disturbing the even tenor of my way (as I think someone may have said before me).

Each day still began much alike. I brewed up, fried a couple of rashers and a round of bread and emptied my slops from the window into a nettle patch. Then I climbed down to go behind the lilac bushes (one wary eye on the scythe) and, afterwards, using Elijah Fletcher's tomb as my wash-stand, shaved. By this time Moon was stirring and waiting for me to go across and have a mug of tea – we'd made it a rule not to make a start on the work until the first flat clang of the elementary school's bell.

Once we got on the job we worked hard enough – but for a shortish mid-day break – until six or seven in the evening. Up on my platform I used to warily circle my quarry (if that isn't too dramatic a way of putting it) in my mind's eye trying first this and then that for, in my job, there can't be a second shot. In fact, usually for several minutes, I'd sit cross-legged like a Hottentot and *think* my way through the day's work.

Anyway, a couple of days after my visit to the Keaches, I was going through this performance when Kathy Ellerbeck made her normal noisy entrance. "Hello up there, Mr Birkin!" she called, "I haven't come to bother you." Then she seated herself in a pew which caught the sunlight.

"People always tell me that before they *do* begin to bother me," I said. "So say what you've come to say and then I can get on. And why aren't you at school? And why didn't we hear the bell this morning?"

"We've broken up," she cried. "For a month!"

"Far too long," I said. "But you can always help your mother."

"Mam says she doesn't see how you can make a living at your job," she said. "She says there can't be all that many pictures hidden on walls."

"Well I don't make much of one," I said.

"One what?"

"Much of a living. Isn't that what we're talking about?"

"Well then," she said. "Why don't you change your job and stay on at Oxgodby?"

I asked her what I should live on. Did she think her Dad would find me a job portering on his station?

"Well, no," she replied. "A porter doesn't need as much education as you have."

"What then?" I asked.

"You could work for the Council like being a rent-collector or a school teacher – you've been to a college."

Not that kind of college, I told her.

"I've asked Miss Wintersghyll and she says, as long as you've been to a grammar school, you could be an ordinary teacher if you get it into your head right from the start that you never could rise to be a headmaster." And, when I remarked that she seemed very eager for me to remain in Oxgodby, she explained that her parents had taken a liking to me, and also I'd be much missed by others of her acquaintance as I was quite well thought of for my reformative work at the Sunday school, as well as for my hardihood roughing it in the belfry.

"Ah, in that case, I'll think about it," I said. "A teacher eh? With a cane behind the cupboard? Laying down the law. Can you see me at it?"

"No," she admitted. "But I expect I might get used to the idea. And so could you if you set your mind to it. Dad says anybody can do anything if he sets his mind to it."

"Right!" I said. "That's settled then. I like being highly thought of, so I'll set my mind to it. Someday, you'll be able to boast 'It was Little Me changed his ways: he owes it all to Me.' But now I must see about earning the balance of my pay which I confidently believe Mr Keach will hand over any day now."

And so it went on until, after a longer than usual silence, I looked down and she had gone. But she'd put the axe to the very roots of my self-esteem: surely we shouldn't be required, even by worthy Ellerbecks, to justify the ethic of our labour? Our jobs are our private fantasies, our disguises, the cloak we can creep inside to hide. And to be brought to book twice in one week is against natural justice. But I was.

Alice Keach always stayed below too. She would discreetly leave the door slightly ajar and then seat herself in the back pew and shelter behind her wide-brimmed straw-hat (a rose pushed into its band). But for the occasional creak in the scaffold whenever I shuffled back a pace to see what I'd been doing, the building was so still that, although I was a good thirty paces away and my back towards her, we talked casually as we might have talked in a parlour. Not a conventional conversation – no more than a remark, a question, answer, exclamation. Really, there was no need to look: from the way she put things I could see her face.

"How did you come to take up this kind of occupation, Mr Birkin?" (a mischievous twist to her lips, a mock innocent gaze). "I mean how did you discover that such a job existed? Was it in the family?"

(If she could have seen Dad in his office at the scented-soap factory, packing his gladstone bag of samples!) "Well, yes, in a way I was, Mrs Keach. How clever of you to guess. We *were* in the cleaning business."

"How very interesting! And did you travel around with your father to pick up the finer points?"

"Oh no – never. He couldn't stand anyone with him when he was travelling. He found the work a strain on his nerves. Always came home in a foul temper. Didn't speak. Went straight down the back garden. Didn't even take off his hat. Cutting down things helped. My mother used to shudder for her roses. The first ten minutes were the worst; anything might happen. Temperament, you follow. All artists have it."

(I was working up the three brothers (see Matt. V.), blissfully heedless of the judgement to come. The second magnate's cloak was a splendid garment – red outside and green lining. A very good red, the best in fact, no expense spared, sinoper haematite that is, not to be confused with what some fatheads call sinoper which, as often as not, is red earth, the stuff they used to bring in by the shipload from Pontus Euxinus (and don't ask me where that was). That's the red which darkens almost as soon as you turn your back on it: it survives and that's all that can be said for it. In fact, on damp walls, it's all that does survive. Well, back to this chap's cloak. It was resin-based and that doesn't ooze out, by the gallon; they found a scallop-shell with a caked deposit amongst rubble in the Gifford Chantry at Boyton.)

Well, there it is, you can't get away from it, if you want quality you have to pay in one way or another. (Vinny had quality and I paid for it all right.)

"I can't see much from down here, Mr Birkin. Please – what are you at now?"

"I'm valeting a gent's overcoat."

"Is it very soiled?"

"Very! You can't beat tallow candles for laying down a nice grease base for other muck to stew in. You modern women don't know you're born."

(The thing that keeps you from screaming . . . well, that's extreme . . . let's say, it helps if you can guess how things once were. What I'm really getting at is that it's not all that easy to find your way back to the Middle Ages. They weren't us in fancy dress, mouths full of thees and thous, quoths, prithees and zounds. They had no more than a few entertaining distractions to take their minds off death and birth, sleep and work and their prayers to the almighty father and his stricken son when things got too awful. So, in my job, it helps if you can smell candles, guttering in draughts, petitioning release for souls in purgatory, if you can see their smoke trailing amongst images, threading nave arcades, settling on corbels and bosses, blackening stone too high for the cleaning women to get at.

I suppose it all sounds airy-fairy but I stick to my point. If you can see or guess at the comings and goings from first daylight to dusk, crouching, nodding, stubbing breasts and heads with fingers just out of the cooking pot, grubby faces staring up at the only picture they'll see till next they see it – well, then you put that bit extra into the job, you go at it with emotion as well as diluted hydrochloric.)

"Mr Birkin . . . Mr Birkin . . . is it an oil-painting or a water-colour or what is it for goodness sake?"

"It's all sorts of things, Mrs Keach. Item – blew bysse at 4s.4d. the pound, item – one sack of verdigris at 12d. a pound, item – red ochre, 3 pounds a penny, item – 3 pecks of wheat flour . . . I suppose you could lump it all as tempera. And let's not forget the wall itself – down in the sinful south, plastered with chalk bound with parish offerings of skimmed milk; up here, slaked-limestone putty damped just enough to stiffen. That's about what it is."

"You're making fun of me. I'm not utterly stupid you know. An aunt once gave me a paint-box for my birthday: I recall it had a marvellous slab of purple." And then that spurt of laughter like a bell.

"I'm not making fun, Mrs Keach. Ask Mr Dowthwaite at the smithy – he understands having to make-do, flatten this, splay that, till it's something not listed in the Ironmongers' Catalogue. My departed colleague's lad (at 10 pence a week) would do his best with a slab of flat marble and scrape his knuckles grinding Spaynishe white, Baghdad indigo, Cornish malachite, terre verte.

And he would need a tin bowl to break the skimpy eggs of his day: I'm told they were no bigger than a wood pigeon's. Naturally he'd suck the yolk before stirring colour into the white. And my departed friend would yell down, 'Hey you, Idle Jack, some more green. Which green? The cloak-lining green, fat-head! The malachite! And look sharp; we're on piece-work. We have to be off to Beverley first thing Tuesday and God knows what the roads will be like in those Holderness swamps.' "

"Poor boy!"

"Lucky boy! He might have been soaking out on the plough-strips. He might have been having his backside whipped at the abbey school. Anyway, you of all people shouldn't spare him a ha'porth of sympathy: he used your husband's altar slab to do his grinding on."

"Good gracious! How can you possibly know what the poor fellow did?"

"Found a tinge of red in an undercut of one of the consecration crosses."

That was how we talked. And, after a longer silence than usual, I would know she had gone.

Before those few weeks of my stay in Oxgodby I hadn't attended a place of worship since I was a boy. Looking back, I think that I became an unbeliever when I was eighteen, well maybe seventeen, and it can't have been a momentous decision. My parents weren't churchgoers but they'd had a church wedding, seen me baptized and, I fancy, believed vaguely in a hereafter. In the season, very early most Sundays, Dad used to go off coarse-fishing. He used to stick his head into my bedroom – 'Just off to praise my Maker on the river bank: look after your Mum.'

Well, up there in the North Riding, I was thrown back

in at the deep-end, on Sundays shaken into consciousness when Mossop began to toll the bell above me, although I immediately shut my eyes again – the rope slipping up and down through my floor and ceiling made me giddy. And then half-hearing Keach's eucharistic rites oozing up round the baluster. The evenings found me roaring away in the Ellerbeck pew with the Wesleyans because, although I had a standing invitation to have a bite of supper any Sunday at the station-house, I felt conscience-bound to earn my keep by turning up at the chapel. Frankly, I'm not at all sure that, once I got into the swing, if I didn't enjoy it. Yes, I *enjoyed* it.

It was a livelier performance than Keach put on. To begin with there was a different preacher each time – clerks, shop-keepers, one even was a yeast-salesman. But mostly they were pretty rough stuff, farmers or their labourers, men who'd left school at twelve or thirteen. Their convictions were firm as a bishop's but, employing the vernacular in common usage behind Kilburn and Rievaulx, they might have been preaching in a foreign language, certainly in a tongue my southern ancestors had forgotten. Some of their English was so wild that even Kathy at the harmonium and those of the choir whose faces I could see, choked behind their handkerchiefs.

I remember one old gent extolling his zeal. "T'missus and me, yam's doon a claay laane, a lang claay laane, and roond ooor spot t'claay's claggy. Yan sabbath t'missus says 'Fairther, ah'll nut be gannin ti t'chapel, t'muck'll be ower me beeat tops.' 'Nay,' I says, 'thu maunt let a bit o' muck keeap thee yam, ah'll hump thi on me back an' thu m'clag on till we git ower t'wast o't'claay. . . .' "

Nowadays, I suppose comprehensive schools and the

BBC have flattened that splendid twang with their dread stamp. But then, at the end of the horse age, each purveyor of the gospel had no exemplar other than some earlier preacher he had admired. Indeed, it was so with Mr Ellerbeck himself, who had left a village school at fourteen and had become a local preacher in his late teens. Though the mildest, most self-contained of men, once in the pulpit he became his own father who, it appeared, had been a passionately violent and irrational man.

It's not strictly true that climbing the pulpit stairs transformed him; he was mild enough when announcing hymns and only mildly extravagant in his tediously supplicatory obeisance at his oriental despot's skirts. But once launched upon the waves and billows of his sermon, he roared and raved like a madman, now and then bashing down his big fist on the podium so that the water decanter leapt. The while, his wretched wife hung her head in shame and only her twitching fingers revealed suffering. Mercifully, once at ground level again, he came-to like one revived from a convulsive fit and not remembering it.

Well, after their evening services, it was customary to repair to the station-house's front room where there was an American pedal organ, a fantastic confection with parts which glided in and out, parts that could be squeezed and swung, swell, stops, mirrors, pillared flower stands, elbow-rests for baritones overcome by emotion, four brass candleholders that could be adjusted to cast advantageous light on both singer and song; and all this topped by a fretted parapet behind which glass and pot heirlooms were safely displayed.

Anyway, after Sunday evening service, it was open house around this splendid machine and, between bouts of hymn singing, guests were invited to favour the assembly with a solo. In those long-gone days I rather fancied myself as a light baritone and, when my turn came, sang something that had always gone down well in barracks and clubs. It began,

> 'There sat one day in quiet
> In an alehouse by the Rhine
> Three hale and hearty fellows
> And quaffed the flowing wine . . .'

When I'd finished – and it ran to six verses – the roomful either looked uneasily past my neck, or at the pricked hearthrug: it was disconcerting. At last Mrs Ellerbeck said, "That was very nice, Mr Birkin. But not the drink part of it. It all sounds so romantic, but oh the misery and despair of many a wife and child!" Well, that knocked my end in.

Afterwards, Mr Ellerbeck accompanied me up the lane towards the church. "You mustn't be put out," he said, "Mrs Ellerbeck meant it for the best. Keep it q.t. but her dad was a boozer who didn't know when to stop. You often find them like that, up on the Wolds: it's the Danish blood in them. In fact, *he* had a long fair beard and blue eyes. I don't think he ever liked me.

"Living in London, I don't imagine you know how most of them live in the East Riding. You go from one bedroom into the next, no passages. Then, as likely as not, the last bedroom has the staircase, very steep, no bannisters and a door at the bottom held-to with no more than a sneck. From what they let drop, her dad got up in the middle of the night, in need of the chamber-pot, and drink confused him. So he fell straight down the stairwell and, being a big heavy man, straight through the door."

Good Lord! What a picture! Utter stillness and then this frightful uproar as he banged from side to side clutching at nothing, first smacking down that door and then crashing with it into the black living-room, maybe a chair splintering beneath the avalanche. Then some strangled grunts, then his appalled family staring at the still blue eyes.

"Yes," he went on, "of course I'm against drink, dead against it. But not to my wife's extent."

After that, I used to look at Mrs Ellerbeck with a more speculative eye. Before, she'd been just a pleasant homebody. But now – well, think of it. Cooped up in two or three rooms with this bearded giant who, when he was boozed up, became an unpredictable stranger, her mother struggling to conceal fear and contempt. Then this shattering end in the darkness! Remembering that silly romantic song, I felt terrible. And how lightly the poor woman had let me off because, when I put a hand into my coat pocket, I found a packet of beef sandwiches!

And, at the next gathering around that organ, she mercifully offered me redemption. "Oh, Mr Birkin," she said, "we did enjoy that tune you gave us. Can't you change the words round a bit?" And, to salve my soul, this I did –

'There sat one day in quiet
In a tea-shop by the Rhine . . .'

Only Kathy seemed to see the comical side of it, but she was a merciful girl and never used it against me.

By this time, the apex of the arch and its left-hand side were almost uncovered. The notabilities had been given notable treatment; he'd even used gold leaf on the clothes and, astonishingly, cinnabar to gladden lips and cheeks of the supporting seraphic cast. In fact, here and there, the willingness of whoever had put up the money had gone to his head and he'd been staggeringly prodigal with the expensive reds and almost prohibitively priced leaf.

But once he'd begun (as I was now beginning) on the damned souls dithering on the brink of the flames or hurtling headlong into them, he'd switched to the cheap stuff, red earth and iron oxides. Even so, this concentration of similars saved it from odious comparison with the no-expense-spared Michael and his bloodthirsty furnace-hands. And he'd compensated too by his vigorous treatment: he'd really warmed to the work. Up at the top he'd done an extremely competent job, well, more than that, because he was master of his trade and couldn't have done anything but a great job. But now, coming to this lower slope, he'd thrown in the lot – art and heart.

So, each day, I released a few more inches of the seething cascade of bones, joints and worm-riddled vitals frothing over the fiery weir. A few wretches were still intact. To these he hadn't given a great deal of attention; they were no more than fire fodder. All but one. And he, I could have sworn, was a portrait – a crescent shaped scar on his brow made this almost certain. His bright hair streamed like a torch as, like a second Simon Magus, he plunged headlong down the wall. Two demons with delicately furred legs clutched him, one snapping his right wrist whilst his mate split him with shears.

It was the most extraordinary detail of medieval painting that I had ever seen, anticipating the Breughels by a hundred years. What, in this single detail, had pushed him this immense stride beyond his time?

So there I was, on that memorable day, knowing that I had a masterpiece on my hands but scarcely prepared to admit it, like a greedy child hoards the best chocolates in the box. Each day I used to avoid taking in the whole by giving exaggerated attention to the particular. Then, in the early evening, when the westering sun shone in past my baluster to briefly light the wall, I would step back, still purposefully not letting my eyes focus on it, then I looked.

It was breathtaking. (Anyway, it took my breath.) A tremendous waterfall of colour, the blues of the apex falling, then seething into a turbulence of red; like all truly great works of art, hammering you with its whole before beguiling you with its parts.

One evening, I was so lost in it that I didn't hear Moon climb the ladder and yet wasn't startled finding him by me. When, after a few moments, he spoke, it was plain that he, too, had been lost in it.

"Of course, you know this is going to make a stir when the word gets around?" he said. I nodded. "Is there anything anywhere else like it? In the same league?" No, I told him, there wasn't. Once, yes. But no longer. Croughton, Stoke Orchard, St. Albans, Great Harrowden – they'd all been splendid in their day. But not now.

"Look," he said. "Look at the faces. They're oddly alert. You could swear they're real people. Well, *were* real people. Those two herdsmen angels, the ones with the whips: I swear they're dancing. Amazing! Do you know, in some ways, it brings back the whole bloody business in France – particularly the winters. Those red evenings when the barrage was starting up and each man wondered if this was to be the night. . .

'And he shal com with woundes rede
To deme the quikke and the dede'"

I didn't see it like that. No doubt I didn't want to. Oxgodby was another world: it had to be. To me, this was just a medieval wall-painting, something peculiar to its time and nothing more. Well, we all see things with different eyes, and it gets you nowhere hoping that even one in a thousand will see things your way. So I just told him that, if this one was different, it was because it had been painted by one man, as compared say with Chalgrove where it is believed the drawing was done by the master painter but the colouring had been filled in by assistants. I don't think he was listening.

"I feel terribly smug," he said. "Just the two of us knowing about it before *The Times*'s art critic catches on and signals that here's an iconographic wonder for the academic parasites to suck out the magic. Now it's just ours –

> 'And we each one as we ben here
> In body and soule both I fere
> Shal rise at the day of dome
> And be redy at Hys come . . .'

You know I think I might have stomached religion then; it was grittier stuff."

"There's Alice Keach," I said. "I think she knows too."

He glanced curiously at me and said, "I rather hoped there might be something coming on between you two. No? Pity! She's wasted on Keach."

"I let her come up a week ago. After all, she comes and sits by the door every couple of days and shows an intelligent interest."

"In this? Or you? You've never told me – are you married?"

I told him about Vinny and that she'd gone off with another chap. I didn't tell him that she'd almost certainly bedded down with other men while I was overseas. Nor that she'd left me once before.

"Fair enough!" Moon said. "Feel that we know each other well enough for you not to mind my asking. I've never met the right one myself."

We didn't speak for some time.

"There's a couple of details here might interest you," I said and pointed to the falling man. "He was covered over years before the rest."

Moon shuffled forward and examined him with lively interest. "Yes," he said, "I see what you mean. This crescent scar – one could swear he was meant to be identifiable. But your painter never would have dared. Too bad! It's a riddle without an answer for you, Birkin."

He turned away and stared backwards along the roof, the falling man perhaps forgotten. "Those roof-bosses," he said, "I still stand by my theory that they're not *in situ*. They're from somewhere else. Old Mossop's great-etc-grandad – do you suppose that he had his ear well down in the 1530s – cut off the best bits from an altar-piece and nailed them out of harm's way before the official vandals visited? And while Mossop's in mind, what does he think about your picture?"

I laughed. "He hasn't said, but not much I fancy. But he agrees that, after a couple of months, the congregation will scarcely know it's there. And I'm pretty sure he thinks Keach will have it whitewashed out as soon as I'm on the train. Mossop has a low opinion of his fellow men."

"How does he get on with Keach?"

"Oh, he can answer that for himself. 'Aye weel, Maister Birkin, tha knaws, lad, t'parson gans an' anither cums but us yans clag on 'ere.' "

Then we climbed down and, when I'd had a swill at

the graveyard pump, we went across to his tent and brewed up. It was about seven o'clock and so still I felt that, if someone had spoken a mile away, I could have answered him.

We sat in the warm sunshine: he smoked and I thought about Alice Keach. What with being absorbed in my work and her being *Mrs* Keach, I'd never thought of her except as a charming woman I enjoyed talking to and, given an excuse, looking at. But Moon's speculative enquiry had changed that, and now I found it pleasantly disturbing to consider the possibility of wandering off with her to some quiet room, eating supper, taking her hand, touching her, kissing. An upstairs room, its window open to the smell and sounds of an orchard and, beyond that, fields. And turning towards each other in the dusk. Well, we have our dreams. . . .

"Oh God, here he comes," Moon muttered. "He carries a depressive blight around."

"Good evening!" Keach said, looking uneasy when neither of us answered. "I was just passing. Have you found anything yet, Moon?"

"No," Moon answered.

"Well, I don't suppose for a minute there *is* anything to find. Poor Miss Hebron was not quite herself towards the end."

Moon didn't reply. Keach looked helplessly about him. "Mmmmm," he said half-heartedly. "Complete and utter waste of money!"

Moon gazed into the distance.

"It's disgraceful –" this quite savagely. Then he went off.

"However does the charming Alice put up with him?" Moon said. "Imagine having to eat at least three meals a day and *have* to listen to his bleating. And then share a bed!"

"Perhaps he's different at home," I said. "In fact, he *is* different. Anyway, *I* have to listen to him, labouring as I do in his vineyard."

"What does he go on about?"

"Well, for one thing, the church stove."

"You've told me about that. And it was weeks ago; he can't still be talking about it."

"I don't know. No, really I don't. I know that he's talking. But about what I'm not sure. He doesn't seem to expect any answers. In its way, it can be rather soothing."

Moon giggled. "You're a queer devil, Birkin," he said. "What are *you* like at home, I wonder?" (Now that made me think) "But hasn't he a nerve? 'Poor Miss Hebron – she wasn't herself at the end': I bet there was enough of herself to settle him into his place, because he still resents it. Mossop told me she had him weighed up and, right from the start, gave him no change. Come on and I'll show you our benefactor's lair."

We walked along the stream and then across a footbridge, down a lane, turned past a gate covered with a rind of green mould and off its hinges, into an unkempt drive. The house itself, early Victorian, was immense, its walls full of windows and downpipes. It stood amid rose-beds that had become briar patches, rough grazing once lawns, bushes become trees and trees, thickets.

"Miss Hebron is described as greatly resembling her house," Moon murmured. "She either threw her clothes on or slept in them. Mossop tells me she bought several outsize thick skirts at a jumble sale and, one after another, wore them out over several years."

"You'll have to do better than that," I remarked. "You make her sound no more than a bundle of old clothes."

"Very pale eyes – grey I imagine. Her hair kept

changing colour I'm told; once it was orange. Very long thin nose. Her teeth, that's what people mention most. They were extra large and when she smiled . . . Mossop says he found her frown less alarming."

I looked at the decaying house. There must have been thirty rooms, maybe more. And long corridors, staircases, box-rooms, cellars, attics. Poor woman! At night she would have had to go about with a candle, fumbling in the creaking blackness when draughts blew it out.

"She had a sister living with her once, I'm told – Miss Hetty. She normally would have been in an asylum but Miss Hebron wouldn't let anyone examine her."

"And now the Colonel's left on his own?"

Moon nodded. "What are your feelings about growing old, Birkin?"

It wasn't an inconsequential question: I could tell that he really wanted an answer, a second opinion.

"I can't imagine," I said. "I mean I can't imagine it happening to me," I said. "It's too far away now. Well, do you wonder? You know what it was like. There can't have been many of us who thought we'd need to worry about growing old."

"Or what comes after?" he said.

> "'Whoso has don well schal go to blysse
> Whoso has don evil to peyne I-wysse'?"

"Oh come on," I said irritably. "We went in and we came out. That's good enough for me. We're here on borrowed time, and I'll take what's to come as it comes."

Day after day that August, the weather stayed hot and dry. These days we call it real holiday weather but, then, only the well-to-do in those parts went far afield and even a week at Scarborough was remarkable. Folk stayed at home and took their pleasure from an agricultural show, a travelling fair, a Sunday school outing or, if they had social pretentions, a tennis party with cucumber sandwiches. Most country people had a deep-rooted disinclination to sleep away from home and a belief that, like as not, to sojourn amongst strangers was to fall among thieves. It was the way they always had lived and, like their forefathers, they travelled no further than a horse or their own legs could carry them there and back in a day.

And this steady rhythm of living and working got into me, so that I felt part of it and had my place, a foot in both present and past; I was utterly content. But I didn't know this until, one day, Alice Keach said, "You're happy, Mr Birkin. You're not on edge any more. Is it because the work is going well?"

Of course, she was right. Anyway, partly right. Standing up there on the platform before a great work of art, feeling kinship with its creator, cosily knowing that I was a sort of impresario conjuring and teasing back his work after four hundred years of darkness. But that wasn't all of it. There was this weather, this landscape, thick woods, roadsides deep in grass and wild flowers. And to south and north of the Vale, low hills, frontiers of a mysterious country.

I had my dinner with the Ellerbecks each Sunday now. Perhaps they'd talked it over and weighed me up as an amiable wanderer who might be brought back to the fold. Who knows? Perhaps they merely liked me and felt that they needn't stand on ceremony when I was their guest. Anyway, I recall one particular meal early in August. We'd finished the main course (they didn't serve a sweet pudding on Sundays) and were drinking our tea when Mr Ellerbeck, with no more than a hint of holy martyrdom in his tone, remarked, "Well, it's Barton Ferry for me this afternoon, Mother."

"The Superintendent shouldn't have planned you then," his wife exclaimed indignantly. "He's planned you for Malmerby for their six o'clock. Planning you for morning and evening in different chapels is bad enough, but afternoon and evening is over much. And Ferry!"

"Poor little Ferry!" Mr Ellerbeck said, showing no inclination to hasten there. "Well, we have to keep those little spots going, and chapel is about all that ever happens there."

"You're tired out," Mrs Ellerbeck said fiercely. "At your age you should be having a lie-down, not pedalling down that long road."

"And the wind always against you, whether you're coming or going; you always say so," Kathy put in, rooting her dad more firmly in the armchair. Feeling something was expected of me, I made a mournful noise.

"Perhaps Tom here will go for you," Mrs Ellerbeck said resourcefully, turning on me and knowing that, after one of her splendid dinners, I was defenceless. "There'll be only two or three there."

"Yes," Kathy said pitilessly. "There's nothing to be afraid of, is there, Dad? You said yourself there was nobbut a great farm lad, two or three kiddies and Lucy Sykes on the organ. With all your education, Mr Birkin, you can deal with that poor little lot?" She made me sound like a fair-to-average all-in wrestler.

Mr Ellerbeck did not rush forward to succour me. Instead, he looked quizzically at me, only committing himself as far as "Well, there's no denying that Tom's legs are younger than mine."

"You can have Dad's bike," Kathy said, advancing

rapidly into the breach. "It's a three-speed and the chain has an oil bath."

The assault's development had been far too rapid and my defences too over-run for me to mount more than a makeshift counter-attack. "I've never done anything in that line," I protested. "Preaching! Or praying! Praying aloud, that is." (Conscience compelled "aloud" because I'd prayed eloquently enough in my signal-pit during big strafes. And had I felt disposed to reproduce one of those very particular prayers, it would have been the most remarkable utterance heard in *any* chapel, let alone Barton Ferry.)

"You can tell them what you're occupied with," Kathy said. "They'll be very interested because they've got nothing like it in Ferry."

"But the praying. . . ." I mourned.

"The Lord will put words into your mouth," Mr Ellerbeck said, abandoning his neutral position to carry the day.

Well the Lord vouchsafed me no answer to that, and, as token of my unconditional surrender, Edgar (who very decently had preserved impartiality) found me a pair of bicycle clips.

Until then, I'd always been rather fond of Edgar.

Barton Ferry lay four long miles distant along a featureless road. Farmhouses along the way stood a field's length back, and a broad dyke carrying seepage from ditches and drains followed the dusty way to where it stopped at the river's brink. There were a few cottages, a bell on a stout post which also restrained a rowing boat and, on a patch of grass sprinkled with ducks' feathers, a brick chapel scarcely bigger than a large room.

I'd arrived in good time but a brown-faced young woman, a fine healthy child-bearer, was waiting by the door. She was pretty but terribly shy, and gazed away over the river and the road beyond, as I explained lamely that Mr Ellerbeck was off-colour and that I was his inadequate reserve. She made no comment but neither did she seem overly cast down by this news as she let me in and asked for the hymn numbers. I said I'd leave them to her but would be obliged if she'd pick long ones and, preferably, with choruses between each verse.

There were only half-a-dozen pews and these huddled before an enormous varnished pulpit which I scaled and found my exalted position afforded an excellent view of the river through the rear window. Behind my head an enormous clock would share, perhaps engross my fellow worshippers' attention. Then I busied myself finding two very long chapters in the Old and New Testaments and put the tasselled markers in. The clock's loud ticking was much slower than my heart beats. The organist made no sound at all, her strong brown hands on lap, her head hanging. I don't think she was praying. It was very hot and I began to sweat.

On zero hour and not a second earlier, two freckled children, a red-faced farm lad and an elderly man trooped in and penned themselves like sheep below me. I then announced the first hymn, 'O for a thousand tongues to sing my great redeemer's praise', which we sang surprisingly loudly for so tiny a band. The succeeding prayer limped from despairing silence to silence, the Lord signally not honouring Mr Ellerbeck's guarantee on His behalf to put words into my mouth. Nevertheless I stumbled on, tossing in pleas to be forgiven for unmentionable sins I felt were His responsibility (with Passchaendaele in mind) rather than mine, and sprinkling around plenty of Thees and Thous as cover: I deceived nobody. Opening my eyes once, I saw the organist's bowed shoulders were twitching slightly.

After we bellowed hymn 4 ('Crown him with many crowns') I basely determined that I must abandon my awful impersonation, even if I did land the station-master in trouble with the Circuit Authority. "Look here," I declared quite fiercely. "I'm just filling in and, as I've not preached before and certainly shan't again, I'm going to tell you what I'm doing in Oxgodby and, if you want to leave or nod-off, that's alright by me." Actually, they recognised the good sense of this and listened with great attention and, in fact, the children put up their hands and asked several sensible questions. Afterwards, the old boy who was their grandfather said he'd drive them over in his trap so they could see what I'd been talking about.

When they'd drifted off on their several ways I thanked my organist and, as she was locking the door, made to put on my bicycle clips. "You could come on home for your tea," she said.

"Well, I'm expected back I think," I said but then thought, "Why not? Perhaps I can ask her to meet me again." (I was missing a woman badly). So I added, "But I'd like to come; I need a cup of tea in this heat; I know the Ellerbecks will understand."

She lived at a farmhouse gable end to the road – not a big place. Deep red hollyhocks pressed against the limestone wall and velvet butterflies flopped lazily from flower to flower. It was Tennyson weather, drowsy, warm, unnaturally still. Her father and mother made me very welcome, both declaring they'd never met a Londoner before. They gave me what, in these parts, was called a knife-and-fork "do", a ham off the hook, a deep apple-pie and scalding tea. In conversation it came out that I'd been Over There (as they called it) and this spurred them to thrust more prodigious helpings upon me. Then I noticed a framed photo of a young soldier on the piano top.

"That's our son, our Perce," Mrs Sykes said. "He had it taken on his last leave, on his nineteenth birthday." A glance across those faces made it unnecessary to ask what had befallen Perce. But, when I got up to go, I went across and looked more closely at him; he'd been a stocky youth, open-faced, a pleasant-looking chap. His father came up beside me and was looking over my shoulder. "He was a right good lad, Perce," he said, "a real worker. Would give anybody a hand; they all liked him."

And on my way home by the dyke-side, on the empty road between fields of corn blowing like water, I suddenly yelled, "Oh you bastards! You awful bloody bastards! You didn't need to have started it. And you could have stopped it before you did. God? Ha! There is no God." Two horses grazing over a hedge looked up and whinnied.

"How did you get on over at Ferry?" Mr Ellerbeck asked when, that evening, he walked in from Malmerby.

"Well, I learnt one thing," I said "– that I'm not cut out for a preacher. I expect your Super will be round to tick you off when complaints come up the line with the rations."

"He had his tea at Lucy Sykes's," Kathy cried. "She asked him in. He's been quiet ever since, because he's fallen in love with her."

"She's a fine strong girl," Mr Ellerbeck said. "And she gets a lot out of that old organ at Ferry. Good Christian upbringing, too. We'll ask her over to the Sunday-school anniversary and that'll give you another chance to have a look at her."

It never seemed to have occurred to the Ellerbecks that I might have been married.

In London I'd sometimes exchanged a word with the family next door on one side and nodded to the couple on the other but, if I'd passed whoever lived beyond that, I shouldn't have known them. Yet here, within twenty-four hours of my performance at Barton Ferry, word had got around about tea at the Sykes's.

"Hear you're haring round the countryside looking over the girls. Think of settling down in Oxgodby then?" Moon said slyly. "Better keep it quiet that you're wed: every second chap round about has a shot-gun."

Even Alice Keach had heard, but she put it more obliquely at the end of a conversation that had begun by her asking if I'd wanted to be an artist.

"No," I said. "Never thought of it. Didn't know what I wanted to be. I only knew what I *didn't* want to do. I didn't want to be an engine-driver, a policeman or a rent-collector or have anything to do with the sea."

"What about the Church? You would have made a good clergyman."

"Good heavens! Really! That's almost the last thing I'd be any good at. Not my style at all."

"But you would have listened. You *do* listen. And you know how to be still. Don't you know that, when people are with you, they don't feel they have to say something? I mean just say anything to fill in silences. Were you always good at listening? When you were a little boy?"

"My sisters used to say my ears were too big: that meant that I was *too* good a listener. I'm sorry – I know that's not what you mean. Well then, maybe I was. My mother was a quiet woman. She'd sit for an hour sewing or darning and not a word. Sometimes she'd pucker up her mouth and glance at one or the other of us. And, if anything had upset that one at school, she'd hear it all out and then ask one or two questions so, in the end, you found you'd answered yourself. Is that what you mean?"

"Yes," she said. "That's exactly what I mean; I should like to have known her. And Mr Birkin – back to parsons. I hear you were a Great Success at Ferry. . . ."

She said this as she rose from the pew to go. "And that you've fallen in love." She'd gone before I had time to reply; her gay laughter slipped back through the open door.

Well, she was right. I'd fallen in love. But not with sweet Lucy Sykes.

You might wonder what I thought about during the many hours I spent up on that scaffold. Well, obviously, the work itself, the vast painting I was uncovering. But also about the nameless man who'd stood where I stood. Not his technical abilities although, quite properly, these were extremely interesting to me. For instance, he had a very very good line in hands, his speciality being knuckles and wrists. His hands spoke to each other and were answered. But he wasn't much good at feet. Let's leave it at that. No, it was his quirks which really fascinated me. As when, for instance, he'd dropped iconographic rules to slyly lift the line of a man's lips or turned aside to rattle off a string of grace notes on a costume's edge – things just done for the hell of it.

And there always was the enigma of this final falling

man. Simon Magus? The man who'd tried to buy the Holy Ghost? His torments were well documented; the Establishment had seen to that. Keep to the Party Line. Or Else! But, if he was that famed apostate, why had he been painted with so much verve, and why had he been blotted out so much earlier than the rest? And why, why plunging into hell, was he *himself*? Had the painter known him? Was it a portrait recognizable to kinsmen, who had hidden him from public view almost before the paint was dry? Well, it was several hundred years too late to ask now.

"How are you two getting on together?" Moon would say, waving a hand at my wall. "Do you ever feel him breathing down your neck, nudging you – 'Good lad, Birkin! Attaboy!' You must know him pretty well. Go on – tell me about him. Who was he?"

Who was he! I couldn't even name him. People don't seem to understand those far off folk. They simply weren't us. Our idea of personal fame was alien to them. This man of mine, for instance, knew nothing of earlier artists, so why should he suppose anyone would want to know anything of him? So it wouldn't even occur to him to sign his work. Of the hundred, yes at the least a hundred wall paintings, I knew of only a single signature – Thomas of Malmesbury at Ampney Crucis.

And the idea that his work might be minutely observed five hundred years after his death would have been preposterous. In his day, buildings were being drastically remodelled every fifty years as fashions changed, so that my man would calculate his painting, at the longest, would last no more than a couple of generations.

"What did he look like?"

Ah now, that was different. I couldn't put a face on him. But he was fair-headed; hairs kept turning up where his beard had prodded into tacky paint, particularly the outlining in red ochre which he'd based in linseed oil. There was no mistaking it for brush hair which was recognizable from its length, an inch, never more than an inch and a half. Sow's bristle for the rough jobs, badger's grey for precision.

"Mm – quite impressive. And what else can be established about our departed brother?"

"Right handed, about your build – he had to use some sort of stool to get up to six feet – that's if I'm right about the parts he did on his knees or crouched on his haunches. That's about all. Well, maybe he'd lived in some monastery. Only a guess, but his hands talk like monks' hands must have talked in the long silences. Oh, one last thing – he didn't trust his apprentice. He did the lot except this bottom bit, this corner of hell. Look, you can see; it's a rough job, a fill-in. Can't understand why he handed over to his lad when his nose was at the winning-post."

"More than I can tell from my damned stones," Moon said. And went.

Ah yes, this was his Great Work. Whatever he'd been employed on before must, could only have been a work-out for this. He'd sweated here, tossed in his bed, groaned, howled over it. Those torn hands, those agonized fingers,

'And he shal com with woundes rede ...'

And then I knew why that last yard of fire wasn't his. This was his last job. He'd had enough, could stick it no longer. He'd left, thrown in his hand. But in those days you couldn't leave; they'd have hauled him back and kicked him to a conclusion. So he must have died on the job. But his last brush-strokes had been steady and sure, he'd been as fit at the end as when he'd begun.

And then I understood. I turned and, shuffling to the scaffold's edge, stared down at the stone-slabbed floor. He'd fallen.

Great God! I scrambled down the ladder and ran from the church. Moon had almost reach his tent. "He fell," I yelled after him. "This was his last job. He fell."

Moon turned and, as it sunk in, he grinned. "O.K.," he called back. "Mind your own step, then."

Alice Keach came next day about tea-time, but I only knew when I heard someone on the ladder. "Too late again to stop me," she said, "I'm here." Then she didn't speak for some time. I'd have been astonished if she had: at close quarters, face to face, my wall was daunting and she was daunted. I heard her draw in breath. Then she said, "Do you believe in hell, Mr Birkin?"

Now that was a thought! Hell? Passchendaele had been hell. Bodies split, heads blown off, grovelling fear, shrieking fear, unspeakable fear! The world made mud! But I knew it was bible hell she had in mind, hell that went on and on, an aching timeless hell. So I answered, "Well, it depends. Hell's different things to different people and different things to the same person at different times."

She didn't question this: I swear she read my mind. She *knew*. "Then what about hell on earth?" she said.

I told her I'd seen it and lived there and that, mercifully, they usually left an exit open. Then neither of us spoke for a longish time, and I thought that there might be something to be said for seasons in hell because, when we'd dragged ourselves back from the bloodiness, life had seemed brighter than we'd remembered it. We sloughed off the pals who'd gone down into death. While it was day that is. At night, in the dark, for a time they came back but we wanted no part of what they now were: theirs was another world – hell, if you care to call it that.

And then there was Vinny. That had been a sort of hell. But I'd crawled from its pit and, here in Oxgodby, life had flooded back, tingling to my finger-tips, a world of new people who only knew as much of what had happened to me as I cared to tell them.

"Well?" she said.

"Yes," I answered. "I've been there; I have a map of it in my head, and Mr Moon will bear me out. They kept sending us back there and that hell was worse than this chap's." But even as I spoke, I knew she wasn't answered. It was neither that nor a bible hell had made her ask.

"Oh," she said. "I'm sorry. It was a silly question . . ."

That was the missed moment. I should have put out a hand and taken her arm and said, "Here I am. Ask me. What do you want to know? The real question! Tell me. While I'm here. Ask me before it's too late."

And maybe she knew this because she murmured that she must go and, turning away, climbed down. She's lovely, I thought. She's shy, alarmed easily like a wild animal. How did he get her? Trap her? Overwhelm her? What was it like that first night together? Had he knelt by the bed first? Those dark eyes staring into the darkness of some hotel room. She could scarcely have known what marriage meant before then. Yet who knows – doubtless she saw more, much more in Keach than the rest of us. Nothing's so secret as what's between man and wife.

I followed her down. "I've left you a few fresh eggs,"

she said. Then, when she'd gone off to the village, I went across to Moon's tent and we sat on the grass in the evening sunshine. "Well?" he asked.

"I've been talking over hell with Mrs Keach."

He laughed.

"Do you think about it often?" I said.

He pursed his lips, wrinkled his nose and studied the back of his hand. Then – and this was unusual – he looked directly at me. "Often," he said. "Particularly at night; that's the bad time. Your window's open; you must have heard me." He knew there'd be neither perfunctory sympathy nor questions. "But I tell myself it will be better as time passes and it sinks further back. But now we're different. *We* know. We're men apart. Maybe wives know. Yes, of course, they must. And people do understand. I met a chap who went back to teaching. Like you, he'd been a signaller out in the middle, on his own, with only a wire trailing back to his battery. He told me that, for the first four weeks, if a pupil dropped a desk lid he'd throw himself on the floor. At first they used to snigger. Then they didn't laugh any more, only stared horrified or in pity. Finally they just pretended not to notice.

"Me? In the middle of it I used to think, Well, we're in the shadows now, but they'll have to blow the whistle some day and then, all at once, it'll be different; we'll go from this to that. But, of course, it couldn't be like that, could it? It has to work itself out, so I keep reminding myself that I'm still a bit round the bend and perhaps always shall be." He laughed. "You too?"

It was a question that he didn't expect to be answered: the side of my face had been clicking away as he talked.

"It's not anything like so bad as when you first turned up," he said. I flushed but he went on. "I don't suppose you noticed it happening, but Oxgodby's just about ironed you out."

We sat for a time without speaking. At dusk, a few lads came into the meadow and began larking about; a platelayer crossed, pushing his bike along the path to the station.

"Sometimes, I half wanted it to happen," Moon said. "There were times when I'd had enough. Well, you know that. I mean – when I was sure my nerve would give way and I'd lie down before I was hit. Or worse, wouldn't be able to drive myself over the top. So many had gone, chaps I cared for. Sometimes it seemed that they were the lucky ones. But I remember them less well now . . . they're dwindling."

And I thought of the great picture at the top of my ladder. But theirs was a different hell from ours.

The moon had risen, a slight breeze stirred the shadows of trees across fields of barley, white like water.

"Look here," Moon said. "We need a break. Damn it all we're not wage slaves. They're not pouring money over us. Let's take each day as a dividend for what's past. I'll fix it with Mossop. Tomorrow we'll have a holiday."

So, next day, we downed tools and went off to the big field where Mossop was working. Already it was a day of great heat, the barley heads were brittle and bowed and you could have sworn there was an oven smell in the air. When the dew had dried, the reaper-binder, its sails flickering, the team fresh and skittish, began tossing out sheaves and we started to stook. But heavens, the thistles! After a time I learnt to kick sheaves over until I saw a firm handhold before jamming them, heads together, into the stubble, four or five pairs to a stock. And we went on back and forth across the cracked earth in the growing heat till mid-day, when each sheaf's shadow was no more than a black tip. Then it was dinner-time ("t'Missus's expecting you two gents") and rabbit-and-potato pie put fresh heart into us and carried us on until, at four, "th'allooance" came, greengage pie and scalding tea in a can.

And we finished in the dusk, the first star rising above the dark rim of the hills. Kathy Ellerbeck was waiting in the deep roadside grass by the field gate. "Don't forget it's Sunday School Treat tomorrow," she said. "Mr Dowthwaite's expecting you; there'll be your dafties to keep an eye on."

It was useless to claim that I'd been having a holiday all day. She was remorseless. "What about Mr Moon here?" I asked. "Can't he have a treat too?" But no, he couldn't come. The treat was a reward for service and Moon hadn't rendered any. "Anyway," she said, "he's Church."

"How do you know that?" I asked. "As far as I know he doesn't go anywhere."

"From his twang," she said. "Posh!"

"Oh," Moon said. "So by their vowel sounds shall ye know them? Well what about Charity? Aren't all Christians. . . ."

She had the sense not to admit religion into the argument, young as she was, knowing it pointed the way to all manner of disagreeable conclusions, so he didn't finish his sentence. "It's a Rule," she said. "And, anyway, Mr Birkin's nearly finished his job, whereas you've not found what you're being paid to look for."

"Will Miss Sykes from Ferry be coming along?" Moon asked, by way of a counter-attack.

"They have their own Treat, I expect," Kathy said

shortly. "Don't be late, Mr Birkin. The carts pick up at eight and they don't linger."

Next morning I pinned a note to the ladder, BACK TONIGHT, UNSAFE, and, pushing bread and cold bacon into my mouth, ran across the meadow to the nearest roadside and joined a man and woman waiting with two small boys. I was still panting and munching when, beyond a bend, I heard the clipclop of hooves; even in that horse age, it was a marvellously exciting sound.

And then they came, the morning sun gleaming on their chestnut and black backs, glinting from martingales medalled like generals. Their manes were plaited with patriotic ribbons, their harness glowed – those great magical creatures soon to disappear from highways and turning furrow. Did I know it even then? I suppose not, nor anyone else in Oxgodby. From childhood, they had always known the sound of hooves fitfully beating stable floors in the night hours and the bitter smell of burning horn at the smithy. How could they foresee that, in a few brief years, their fellow sharers of field and road would be gone for ever?

Whilst parents sat in back-to-back state on benches ranged down the middle of the flat four-wheeled carts, the lads and girls dangled their legs over the sides. Our party was hauled up on the second equipage, greeted heartily and told that the confidently expected heat would soon have our jackets off. And so we clattered off, calling farewell to those disqualified by infirmity or alien beliefs from joining us, conscious (as were they) that we were part of the ancient cycle of the farming year and that our passing was token that the harvest was almost in.

Am I making too much of this? Perhaps. But there are times when man and earth are one, when the pulse of living beats strong, when life is brimming with promise and the future stretches confidently ahead like that road to the hills. Well, I was young. . .

We picked up the Ellerbecks at the station – as Chapel Steward he'd been kept a seat at Mr Dowthwaite's right hand on the first rulley – then on to the town where market day slowed us to a walk and, sometimes, a halt, as other wagons manoeuvred on the cobbled square. Farmers' wives stood with baskets of home-churned butter and eggs at their feet or offered for sale early apples, hazel pears, bunches of pinks, whatever country folk had more than enough of in their orchards and gardens. I saw a man swinging a bulldog, its teeth clamped on a bootlace. "Ye'll ha' bother brekking a beeat-laace like this yan if t'dog can't", he cried. And, from another stall, the smell of bread baked that morning reminded me that my hurried breakfast had not quelled hunger.

Then we clattered over a bridge and travelled between fields again. Someone nudged me and a thick beef sandwich was passed over my shoulder. It was Mossop and Mrs Mossop nodding encouragingly at me: I had established a reputation for an invincible hunger.

"What are you doing here?" I said. "You're Church."

"Nay," he replied. "Ay've me feeat i' beeath camps. The lot of 'em ha' git ti come at t'finish ti let me put 'em ti bed."

For me that always will be the summer day of summer days – a cloudless sky, ditches and roadside deep in grass, poppies, cuckoo pint, trees heavy with leaf, orchards bulging over hedge briars. And we rumbled along through it, turning away from a finger-post to Sutton-under-Whitestone Cliff and made for the pantile roofs of Kilburn where a joiner in his yard called to and was answered by an acquaintance in the cavalcade.

"Look yonder, Mr Birkin."

"Where?"

"There!"

And, strolling mildly across a steep grassy escarpment, an immense White Horse, a gigantic enlargement of the sort of horse journeymen painters used to knock out for a couple of sovereigns apiece for proud owners up for the Great Ebor Handicap or the Beverley Selling Plate. Its overlong back and swan neck perpetuated horses of an antique world.

There was a throaty smell blowing off the bilberry shrubs and the withering heather when we disembarked on a sheep-cropped plain high up in the hills. There was no shelter from the sun, but it was dinner-time and the women and girls unpacked hard-boiled eggs and soggy tomato sandwiches wrapped in greased paper and swaddled in napkins. It was Mr Dowthwaite (for you laboured for your prestige amongst the Wesleyans) who built a downbreeze fire of twigs and soon had tin kettles boiling. Then he struck up the Doxology and, when we'd sung it, we settled to some steady eating.

Afterwards, most of the men took off their jackets, exposing their braces and the tapes of their long woollen underpants and astonished their children by larking around like great lads. The courting couples sidled off, the women sat around and talked. So eating, drinking, dozing, making love, the day passed until evening came and the horses were led in from their pasture. Then, as the first star rose and swallows turned and twisted above the bracken, our wagons rumbled down from above the White Horse and across the Vale towards home: the Sunday School Treat was over.

And, when we reached Oxgodby, we heard that Emily Clough had died that afternoon.

Ah those days . . . for many years afterwards their happiness haunted me. Sometimes, listening to music, I drift back and nothing has changed. The long end of summer. Day after day of warm weather, voices calling as night came on and lighted windows pricked the darkness and, at day-break, the murmur of corn and the warm smell of fields ripe for harvest. And being young.

If I'd stayed there, would I always have been happy? No, I suppose not. People move away, grow older, die, and the bright belief that there will be another marvellous thing around each corner fades. It is now or never; we must snatch at happiness as it flies.

I only left Oxgodby once – to visit Ripon. Of course, I had meant to see its Minster while I was in those parts, but doubt if I'd have made the trip if Mr Ellerbeck hadn't made me stir myself. It happened because the Trustees had painfully agreed that they could just about afford to replace their harmonium with an American organ. "Actually, it was hearing tell that Church lot are going to have a new pipe organ," Kathy told me confidentially. "It's alright for them; they don't have to forever be raising money to pay their minister like us," she said bitterly. "*Their* money comes from Away."

"We'd be more than obliged if you'd join us Mr Birkin," Mr Ellerbeck said. "You have a real eye for quality, there's no doubting it; that anybody can tell. And we want the best; well, put it this way, we want the best we can afford. There'll be only the four of us, Mr Dowthwaite, you, Kathy and me."

We went by train and found Mr Baines's Piano and

Organ Warehouse in a back street off the Market Place. He had an impressively comprehensive stock; there must have been thirty pianos, as many American organs and harmoniums and a couple of pipe organs. "It's t'Deputation frev Osgodby Wesleyans come about t'organ," Mr Dowthwaite said, bending forward nervously. "Mr Baines knows all about us; Mr Ellerbeck here wrote a letter to say we were coming on the 2.15."

"Mr Baines isn't with us any longer," a well-turned-out young man said, "I am the new proprietor." He priced our raiment and added, "I suppose it is a *pedal* organ."

I was cast down to recognize a London accent; he had made it sound so shameful a transaction. Then he led us briskly along the gangways between his parade of instruments.

"It's all show," Kathy whispered. "They make folks pay through the nose for these mirrors and brass candlesticks. Whereas it's the noise that's all-important. We've got to watch out for the wheezing you get when the bellows are perished."

My murmur can't have been agreeable enough because she continued shrewdly, "And we'll have to be particularly watchful because he's a blinking southerner." Mercifully she didn't add, "like you."

The proprietor was rattling off some dubious technical jargon while he cleverly managed to imply that he was casting pearls before swine without actually saying so. Frankly, the choice was too lavish, like pushing a feast under a starving man's nose; one moment he is dying of hunger, the next of anxiety. But the descriptive flights became briefer, then downright brusque. Eventually he said brutally: "I expect you're wanting something second-hand." We nodded in shame.

"Then you should have said so," he said dismissively. "You'd better have a look behind that lot over there. We took them in part-exchange from go-ahead churches. I don't know what you'll find. Not much I expect. And please note we do not give any guarantee."

"I suppose it's in order to try one or two out?" Mr Dowthwaite asked deferentially.

He was not answered: the proprietor was already gliding away to greet more promising customers.

Now, once this grand person had gone, Mr Ellerbeck became himself again. His eye brightened and a note of decision returned to his voice. "Now let's have a look at these price-tags," he said, pushing briskly into the corral for despised and rejected instruments. "It's no use trying anything we can't afford. Spread out and then report back."

And we did.

Five minutes later he announced. "Then that's settled and we can get on. It has to be one of these three – this one, the yellow-looking one and that one there. Kathy lass, fetch yon music-stool and let's hear you sound 'em out, one after another." And, having arranged her long hair and jamming her hat on more firmly, that's what she did, putting all three organs and *All people that on earth do dwell* vigorously through their paces. And, whilst she pedalled away like mad, trying combinations of stops and swells, Mr Dowthwaite crouched with his head pressed to the organ's back. "I'm no musician Mr Birkin," he explained, observing my astonishment, "that I freely admit to; but wind, that I do understand and let no man deny it, bellows being, as it were, my business."

As far as I was able to tell the three candidates sounded much alike, and my sole contribution was to point out that one vibrated when worked hard and that a second smelled odd. I therefore was gratified when it was decided that the third was the favourite and thus must be tested to the very limit. However, at this moment, the other customers must have decided on a similar course and began releasing peals of thunder and strident fanfares from what announced itself to be a large, very expensive pipe-organ.

"Go and enquire how long he's going to make that din for, Mr Birkin," Kathy ordered, so I sidled out from the cast-offs and, skirting several thickets of music-making impedimenta, emerged into a clearing reserved for grander clients. And these were the Keaches.

I stopped in my tracks but before I could melt back guiltily into the friendly jungle, Alice Keach turned. At that moment the better to conduct his pneumatic investigation, Mr Dowthwaite mounted a chair, thus explaining my presence. Her eye brightened. For a moment I believed that she would burst out laughing. Perhaps she did. But, at that moment, the proprietor released another blast on his organ and, under cover of its barrage, I retreated.

"They've just about finished," I lied. So, unwrapping the paper parcel he'd been carrying to reveal the Wesleyan Hymnal, Mr Ellerbeck said, "Well, if we're going to catch the 4.7 we'll make a start. Here Kathy, let's have No. 389, 'Lo, He comes with clouds descending once for guilty sinners slain'. It's got plenty of go in it." And with her knees cleverly pushing out both swells and her feet pumping up and down like a sprinter, she produced a respectable counter-blast.

"I think this is it, Mr Dowthwaite," the Stationmaster said. "What about you, Tom? Still, before we finally plump for it, let's see how it sounds with a bit of singing – after all, you only hear an organ on its own twice, when you come in and when you go out. Here – No. 119, Kathy, 'Worthy is the Lamb'."

And off they went; Kathy leading off in an unusually strong soprano howl, Mr Ellerbeck's exaggerated tenor almost harmonising with the blacksmith's basso profundo (both mighty hands across his waistcoat) whilst I examined the ceiling, wondering what Alice Keach was making of the din.

> 'Worthy is the Lamb,
> Worthy is the Lamb,
> Worthy is the Lamb for sinners slain
> For sinners sla-a-a-ain
> For sinners sla-a-a-ain
> Worthy is the Lamb for sinners slai-i-in.'

It was a splendid noise and they were well into verse 3 before a maniacal yell choked them off: it was the proprietor, beside himself with rage. "Here," he shouted, "stop that. You can't have a blasted choir-practice here. My other customers can't hear themselves."

The three songsters tailed off into shamefaced silence.

"We'll have this one," Mr Ellerbeck said. "I'll have it collected by N.E.R." And Mr Dowthwaite recovered his aplomb with splendid élan. "Any discount for cash?" he asked, taking out a pile of soiled notes and a bag of silver. "Let's say a couple of pounds off, cash down."

Business was business to the Oxgodby deputation and, leaving the flabbergasted vendor, off they went to catch the 4.7, dragging their reluctant organ-player with them. But I excused myself, feeling that I couldn't decently leave the place without admiring its Minster. So off I went down the hill to the great rambling barn of a building. But for an ancient verger pottering about, I had the great forest of stone all to myself and, for an hour, pottered and marvelled with him.

Then I shambled back to the Market Place and had buttered teacakes in a room behind a baker's shop. And it was a very good pot of tea, hot and freshly made. I remember the cake too, seed-cake, first rate. Now that's something you'd be lucky to find in London, either then or now. It was a comfortable place to eat, had a well-used feel about it, the sort of place you could sit back in without someone hovering to snatch away the crocks or fill your chair. I lost myself, going over the afternoon, marvelling that I'd been asked to help pick an organ, uncomfortably wondering what Alice Keach had thought, hoping that perhaps, against all the odds, she might slip in here for tea or travel home alone on the 6.20.

I lit a Woodbine. Someone, a customer, another man came in, but I didn't turn until he spoke. "Well, would you credit it? Do you live here?"

At first I didn't recognize him. "Milburn," he said – "Sergeant Milburn." I knew him then; he hadn't been a bad chap. I believe he was a Kitchener volunteer, not a conscript like me. I'd last seen him in a roofless billet at Bapaume. "Last time I saw you they were carting you off," he said. "Let's see – shell-shock, wasn't it? Advance signaller weren't you? Not many of you chaps came through."

He moved over to my table and told me he was a commercial traveller in ironmongery and had good steady connections in the north-east. I told him what I was doing; he sounded amazed that I'd been at L.C.A. before I was called up. "Never would have guessed," he said. "Just took it you were some sort of clerk."

Then I mentioned Moon.

"Moon!" he said. "A stocky chap, reddish faced, spoke lad-di'-dah?" He saw from my face that he had the right man and laughed. "I bet they knocked hell out of him in the glasshouse," he said. "His sort always got it worst. A corporal, who had it in for him, gave the game away: the M.P.s found him in bed with his batman."

It was like a blow in the face but I don't think that he noticed.

"They really shat on him at the Court-Martial. Crucified him. 'Corruption of young men' . . . 'Dishonour of the king's commission' . . . that sort of balls. His M.C. made it worse. Can't understand that."

"He's never mentioned an M.C." I said.

"Immediate award. Brought in one of his chaps from the wire. Went back when he heard another screaming, even though he must have known it was all up with him. Poor bugger! I suppose he was born that way."

Then he said, "Perhaps I shouldn't have told you. Well keep it to yourself. Better not mention we met. Well it was nice running into you. Don't suppose it'll happen again." He pushed out a hand and went.

Knowing Moon was homosexual didn't upset me, though of course it wasn't something I could forget. It was the idea of an independent man, a proud spirit, being shut up like an animal in a military prison and having to put up with the ghastly crew who always seemed to grope their way in to run those places – that's what appalled me.

Of course, it didn't end there. Don't ask how but, from that day, Moon knew that I knew. Next day, for no reason at all, he said, "Sex! It's the very devil. Quite merciless! It betrays our manhood, rots our integrity. Isn't it, perhaps, the hell you were asking about, Birkin?"

And, from that time on, things were never quite the same between us.

*

For a few days now I'd been having a second look at the picture's north side, the last stretch, the glad souls whose virtues had outweighed their iniquity in Michael's scales and now were streaming uphill to their reward. A smug, uninteresting lot they were too, with none of the liveliness of their brethren condemned to the torment. And they hadn't worn well either; their seraphic blues must have started fading during the first twenty years.

So, by and large, the work was near enough done and, if I'd gone off on the instant, no-one would have known the difference, not even old Joe Watterson unless he'd borrowed a ladder. But to satisfy myself, I had to gather up the whole, lightening here, not taking off all the grime there – leaving some perhaps to give body to an outlined limb or to contrast more starkly hair and face. In our business no-one has come up with an instrument that pings when you've cleaned off the grime of time's fell hand and just another touch will shift the hand itself. So I had to fall back on good old rule-of-thumb. It really amounted to looking long and doing little.

The anxious time was over; I was in calm water now. The weather, those long warm days, went on in majestic succession right through August. The front gardens of cottages were crammed with marjoram and roses, marguerites, sweet william, at night heavy with the scent of stocks. The Vale was heavy with leaves, motionless in the early morning, black caves of shadow in the midday heat, blurring the sound of trains hammering north and south.

Summertime! And summertime in my early twenties! And in love! No, better than that – secretly in love, coddling it up in myself. It's an odd feeling, coming rarely more than once in most of our lifetimes. In books, as often as not, they represent it as a sort of anguish but it wasn't so for me. Later perhaps, but not then.

I was married. Vinny had gone off with him but neither of us had done much about it. She'd shrewdly left the door open so that, if need be, she could slip back– before she went again. And Alice Keach. I was sure that she was a deeply religious woman: marriage for her really did mean 'let no man put asunder'. Never forget this was 1920, another world.

So there it was and there it would stay until the day I would go. Then, for a year or two, perhaps we'd exchange a polite Christmas card and, after that, we'd draw further away. But now she was here and, unknowing, mine. Well, that's how I liked to think of it.

She came each day now, aware no doubt that soon Moon and I would be gone and Oxgodby the emptier. Our conversation ranged more widely. She knew about Vinny, the haphazard way we'd lived, what seemed to have gone wrong. We even talked about the chap himself and how, oddly, I still rather liked him.

"I don't know how you can laugh at it, Mr Birkin," she said.

"Two months ago I wouldn't have laughed," I answered. "That's what Oxgodby's done for me. If going off with him is what she needed, then why not? I'm not her jailer. We didn't really know each other when we married. Who does? For that matter, who knows all that much about anyone even after twenty years in the same house? We only show what we care to and so it's a bit of a guessing game, isn't it? And if the other person doesn't care to answer 'Right' or 'Wrong', guessing it stays."

But she didn't take this up. Instead, she told me of her schooldays in Hampshire, how she'd been very close to her father, went everywhere with him, and then he'd died and, a year afterwards, she'd married. And this time *I* changed the subject.

I recall her coming in the day after my trip to Ripon, when I still was thinking over what I'd been told about Moon. "I think you're not listening to me, Mr Birkin," she called up. "Would you like me to sing to you?" And she began in a fair approximation of broad Yorkshire,

> 'For sinners sla-a-a-ain
> For sinners sla-a-a-ain
> Worthy is the Lamb for . . .'

and broke off into giggles, then delicious peals of laughter.

"Be still," I said. "That's a raw spot. Besides, I've something on my mind."

"So you're not working?"

"Oh yes I am. I'm *looking* at it. You have to keep an eye on a picture or anything might happen. It might disappear again before your husband feels he's got his moneysworth."

"Don't, please!" she said.

"You're right, sorry! Stupid thing to say!"

"My husband . . ." she began and then was silent for a few moments. She tried again. "Arthur – in a village it's not easy. He's a very sincere man. He thinks that, perhaps, we'd fit in better further south. He has a sister and brother in Sussex. . . ." It sounded like a cry for help. "I like the people here," she went on, "but I'm not sure they care much for us. We don't fit in."

"Oh you're wrong," I said.

"Do you think so? Really?"

"I know many local folk would be sorry if you ever decided to flit."

"Flit?"

"It's what they call moving house. Rather a nice way of putting it. Why, you're even a hit with the Wesleyans," I said, feeling she needed a boost. "Mrs Ellerbeck says you're very attractive. Now what about that? From another woman at that!"

"Attractive!" she said, as though this had never occurred to her or that no-one had told her so before.

I moved to the edge of the platform and looked down.

"You *are* attractive," I said.

"Attractive?" she repeated helplessly. Many women would have explored this. Not too far, but far enough to leave room for retreat and come away unscathed.

All right Alice Keach, I thought, you're going to be pushed. *You* can lie awake in the dark too.

"Many men would say you are more than attractive," I said. "They'd say you were beautiful." (I stopped short of 'I').

"Oh," she said, looking wildly for succour to Laetitia struggling up from her tomb, knowing safety lay in retreat from the building but not how to decently withdraw. Then she rallied and counter-attacked.

"And you?" she said.

"Me! Well, I'm not an artist, but they gave me a diploma at L.C.A. with a cast-iron guarantee that I could be relied upon to recognize Beauty whenever my eyes fell thereon. So, professionally, I must tell you, Yes, you're beautiful. Very." And could she have made herself go that little bit further and given me the nod, I would have recited a catalogue of her charms – in detail – because my blood was up. *Delectissima, amantissima*!

But fate in the preposterous guise of Mossop stepped in. "Ee, Maister Birkin," he bawled, "Ah've 'eeard thoo's at tag-end and'll be gannin yam enny daay noo."

"Would you like me to translate, Mrs Keach?" I called down.

But she'd gone.

Vale.

I don't know what Alice Keach told her husband but, first thing next day, he was in the building when I got back from my mug of tea with Moon. "Mossop tells me the work is done," he said before I'd scarcely crossed the threshold. "Yes, I see it is. Very good. So the executors have authorized me to make the final payment. It's here in this envelope. £13.15s. as we agreed."

There had been a blank wall and now it wasn't blank. There had been the nuisance of a scaffold and a man living in his belfry who now could be packed off. Great God, the vast creative process was hidden from him. And us – the long-dead wall-picture painter – and myself, who'd laboured to drag his picture back into sight . . . neither of us had meaning for him. It was that, as much as anything, that made me tell him that I should need the scaffolding for several more days.

"But you have finished," he said. "And now you have been paid."

"*You* said I was finished," I answered. "And I didn't ask for the money."

"You have taken several holidays," he said. "An entire day in the harvest field and another with the Wesleyans and, on several occasions when I've called, you've not been here."

"Look Vicar," I said sharply, "I'm not being paid by the hour or the day and lucky for you that I'm not. The job's not finished."

"I shall have the scaffolding removed," he said stubbornly.

"Oh, will you," I said. "Then I shall inform the executors that you've prevented me completing my contract and no doubt that will relieve them from forking out the thousand pounds Miss Hebron left to the church – conditionally."

He got the message and that I meant it. "I should not wish to quarrel with you, Mr Birkin," he said. "You will not be with us much longer so, if you wish the scaffolding to remain for a few days longer, it can remain. Doubtless you will be kind enough to inform me when I can ask the contractor to dismantle it."

We faced each other for a few moments without speaking. My anger had gone; I just wanted him to go away. But when he spoke, curiously enough he used the same words as his wife. "It's not easy," he said. "I wasn't always, well, not as I may appear to be."

I tried to look as though I didn't know what he was talking about and, finding this not too successful, looked as though I was astonished that everyone didn't see him as a fine dynamic saintly fellow, venerated by his flock and marked for glorious ascension into canonry and even beyond. Again I can't have succeeded because he smiled. Bleakly – but it was a sort of smile. "I know how you see me. Moon too. That's how you want to see me, isn't it? You've made up your minds."

To say the least, this was embarrassing. In part, because people one doesn't care for, even dislikes, make most of us feel uneasy when they appeal against their sentence. And partly, because he was right: we *had* cast him in the role of a sour paymaster who we hoped would go away and be a long time coming back.

"It's not easy," he repeated. "The English are not a

deeply religious people. Even many of those who attend divine service do so from habit. Their acceptance of the sacrament is perfunctory: I have yet to meet the man whose hair rose at the nape of his neck because he was about to taste the blood of his dying Lord. Even when they visit their church in large numbers, at Harvest Thanksgiving or the Christmas Midnight Mass, it is no more than a pagan salute to the passing seasons. They do not need me. I come in useful at baptisms, weddings, funerals. Chiefly funerals – they employ me as a removal contractor to see them safely flitted into their next house." He laughed bitterly.

"But I am embarrassing you, Mr Birkin," he said. "You too have no need of me. You have come back from a place where you have seen things beyond belief, things which you cannot talk of yet can't forget, but things which are at the heart of religion. Even so, when I have approached you during your stay here, you have agreed that it is very pleasant for this time of year, you have nodded your head and said that your work is progressing well and that you are quite comfortable. And you have hoped that I shall go away."

All this time unusually he was looking directly at me. Then he held out the envelope and went. Christ!

That night as we walked back from the Shepherds' Arms I told Moon of Keach's visit. "Well, old boy, I can see his point," he said. "After all, the building's his place of business and you've blocked off a good third of the working area. And besides he's right – you've finished. . . ."

He didn't let me work up a protest. "Oh, come off it. Of course you have. You know you could do what's left to be done in a half-day if you cared to. One only needs to look at you, let alone the wall. For a week now you've been ga-ing roond like a hoond wi twa ta-a-ails (even Mossop's noticed). You're like anyone would be who finds himself landed with a tricky job and pulls it off without putting a foot wrong. Whatever you're hanging about for, it's not to finish *that* job. You can't make it last for ever."

"I don't need to be told," I said.

"For goodness' sake," he said irritably, "I don't mean that and you know I don't, you cagey devil. I mean here, Oxgodby, the friends you've made, this marvellous summer, the splendid job you've done. I mean the lot. You can only have this piece of cake once; you can't keep on munching away at it. Sad, but there it is! You'll find that, once you've dragged yourself round the corner, there'll be another view; it may even be a better one."

He looked quizzically at me. "You've dug in pretty deep haven't you? The Ellerbecks . . . Alice Keach. . . ."

"What about you?" I said.

"Yes, it's time I was off too. I'll give you a couple of days' start just for the look of the thing. Anyway it's autumn tomorrow or the next day: I can smell it in the air – summer smouldering."

"But you've not done what they'll pay you for."

He laughed. "If I'd have done that we'd never have met, should we? Well, I've done what *I* came to do and all that's left is to write it up, which can be done later anywhere. So now it actually has come round to Piers's turn, and I really do believe dear old Miss H. is going to have her moneysworth." He grinned. "As a matter of fact, I rather held my hand until you didn't have an excuse not to lend me one. Tomorrow's the day, my boy. Goodnight."

Just before I bedded down I stood at the window. And he was right – the first breath of autumn was in the air, a prodigal feeling, a feeling of wanting, taking, and keeping before it is too late.

Next morning he routed me out, shouting that I was to have breakfast with him. And then, when we'd eaten, he produced what he called Dowthwaite's Divining Rod, a long steel shaft with a very sharp point the blacksmith had made for him. And, with a shoeing hammer and a grocer's box, we sallied forth.

"The commonality were launched in a shroud," he said. "Pure wool by Act of Parliament to bolster trade. But my man would rate a stone box. That's why we need our Dowthwaite Diviner; it's to take soundings."

He had it all worked out and we took up positions at his best bet, the depression he'd claimed to see the day I'd first met him, a stride's length into the meadow from the wall's south side. "It's about as near as they could get him to the altar; I've had my tape-measure out. Well, man is a creature of hope. Your turn first! Up on the box and don't buckle my rod."

You know, it's quite exciting to watch a professional at work if you bother to look. I mean going at a job he does really well. You look at him with new eyes from then on. In this odd sort of way I was seeing Moon for the first time. You see he was amazingly right. First go! He let me do the donkey work, beating in his rod till it reached what he called the hope-zone. Then he took over, striking more gently and, after each blow, putting an ear close enough to hear vibration coming from below.

"Mmmm," he said, "I suppose it could be a boulder deeper than it ought to be" and tapped again. The rod whinnied. "Right, just let me chalk it at ground level, then we'll have it up and try a foot each way."

A foot west the rod went down below the mark and no jarring tremor. A foot east we struck stone again and again a foot east of that.

"This is highly satisfactory, my good man," Moon said, rubbing his hands. "It only goes to show how much there is in folk-memory and let this be a lesson to you to listen to the world's Mossops. Just as it happens, I have a spade to hand and, as a token of my esteem, you shall cut the first sod. In pirate tales, they never know for sure if the treasure chest is there until they spot it. But I shall announce with utter assurance to you and the Waiting World that you will find Piers as deep as this spade is long.

"Doesn't it excite you?" he said. "Digging where someone dug five, six hundred years ago? No? Well, in my simple way, I find it just as enthralling as your undercover job next door. Ah well, perhaps it was too much to hope for. Like everyone else, you have been brought up to expect a pot of gold, or, at the very least, a doubloon. But we diggers keep our palates fresh; a mild deviation of soil tinge is all we need to stir the adrenalin. Pause, my friend: even you must observe that you are throwing up soil which should have been three spits deeper. Splendid!"

It was extremely hot work and I was very pleased when he lowered his rod into the pit and told me to come out. "You've shown yourself a true blue British workman," he said. "Mossop tells me privately that he's giving up the grave-digging branch of vergering what with the rheumatics, dwindling custom and poor pay. With his support and a reference from me the job's yours for the asking; you can grow old in Oxgodby."

He lowered himself into the pit, crouched on his haunches and began carefully to trowel earth into a carpenter's tool-bag which, now and then, I was bidden to haul up. And so on and so on. "Get a move on," I urged. "We'll be all day at this rate and maybe, at the end of it, find an old horse."

"We *shall* be all day," he answered. "This is about where they'd drop things. Come on now, can't you see one of these peasants of yours on his way home, humping his estovers, stopping to have a squint? And, here, look! Something slips from his pouch. And a little lower – a grieving brother at the grave's brim tossing his last farewell with a handful of earth? Someone *must* have loved him. Surely you of all people, living for weeks up there in the air with them, must be thinking medieval?"

And so it went on all morning until we left off for our bread and Wensleydale and a doze in the sun. Then back again. On his way from the field Mossop rolled up and looked sceptically down. Moon explained that he was digging his own grave as he confidently expected to leave life on the following sabbath and Mossop, remarking that us southerners were fair cautions, went on his way. Kathy Ellerbeck came, the Revd. J.G. Keach came, half a dozen lads came, Mr Dowthwaite came, mad Mrs Higarty, dragging her rickety pushchair, came. But they found no more than a deepening hole and departed sorrowing.

When Moon found what he swore was a horn button, we took this as a sign from heaven that we should withdraw to eat the currant teacakes Mrs Ellerbeck had sent me. "Fifteenth century!" he claimed. "Right on target!" But until he'd smoked a pipe he wouldn't press on. "Come, come," he said. "Keep your shirt on. Whatever's there has been there a very long time;

it won't run off for at least another twenty minutes."

So it was close on six when he signalled the Final Probe by sending up his shoes and socks in the bag and, excitement getting the better of him, began brushing away with rapid strokes, so rapid indeed that you might say the stone swam into sight. A carved shaft branched gracefully into whorls of stone raised upon a convex lid, at its head a hand holding the sacramental cup, a wafer poised at its rim.

"I think there's a name," Moon exclaimed. "I'll winkle out the muck. No, on second thoughts, I'll wash it out. Nip over and fetch me the kettle."

When he'd moistened and swilled the stone he brooded awhile shaking his head. "Well?" I said. "Come on. Is it Piers or isn't it?" Instead of replying he climbed out and said, "No name. Well it would have been extraordinary if there'd been one, I suppose. Just *'miserrimus'* – 'I of all men most wretched', I suppose you might put it. Good God, they really had it in for the poor devil. Why, why, why? Ah well. I suppose we'll never know now."

Then he fetched a camera and photographed it from all sides. "For publication!" he explained. "Against the day when I need a job at a university. They don't want to know if you're any good: just what you've published . . .

"Now," he went on, "Let's have a peep inside before you round up the Colonel and make him sign a chit for his ancestor. It's only a matter of shifting the lid a few inches. The two of us can do it."

So we slid into the pit, and I pushed while he pulled, until the great stone pivoted. Then we looked inside. There is nothing frightening nor even sad about the long dead, just dessicated brown bones and a little dust. What else should we expect after five hundred years? All the same, it's exciting to be the first to see again what has been long hidden, and Moon, pushing his face closer to the gap, blew gently into the trough. A puff of dust stirred. "The shroud!" he murmured.

Then he said, "Oh, come on; in for a penny, in for a pound. Let's push, both of us, and then tipple it against the pit side." So we did and the lid budged inch after inch until we could see the full length of the collapsed skeleton. We crouched and peered at it.

"Excellent condition! Really first-class," Moon muttered. "It must have been absolutely air-tight. But look – see it – third rib down." He bent lower and blew. "There!"

A metal thing swung from the rib-cage; he poked in a pencil and delicately fished it out. "Well, well, the crescent! So that was why they wouldn't let him into the church. He was a Muslim. Caught in some expedition and then became a convert to save his skin! Heavens! Can you imagine the ructions when he turned up in Oxgodby again! Now what's the Colonel going to say?"

He looked quizzically at me. "Too bad!" he said. "But what say that we let sleeping dogs lie, particularly heretic dogs?" and he eased out the chain, snapped a link and dropped it into a handerchief. Then he climbed out, handed down a steel tape and had me call out measurements like a tailor's boy.

"Now," he said, "you round up Keach and I'll alert the Colonel and we'll show off our Exhibit A. Then we'll put the chain back and leave him with his reputation no worse than it was before. But first we'll climb your ladder and have a look at his face before it fell off."

Do you know, until that moment, it hadn't occurred to me that this bundle of bones was my falling man.

*

The next day was Saturday and, now that Moon was done, I decided to bring the job to its end. So I sent word that I shouldn't be able to umpire for the team at Steeple Sinderby and, after working through the morning, came down about two o'clock. I took my bread and cheese outside, half hoping Moon would be about. But he wasn't and, later, I found that he'd gone to York on the morning train.

So I sat on Elijah's tomb slab and, when I'd eaten and smoked a Woodbine, fell asleep sprawled across the warm stone, one arm behind my head. When I awoke, Alice Keach must have been there for some time because she was smiling. "I thought I'd find you here," she said, "when I saw you weren't with the cricketers waiting by the Shepherd. I've brought you a bag of apples. They're Ribston Pippins; they do well up here; I remember you saying you liked a firm apple."

We talked about apples. It seemed that her father had been a great apple man. In Hampshire, they'd had a fair-sized orchard planted with a wide variety and he'd brought her up to discriminate between them. "Before he bit into one, he'd sniff it, roll it around his cupped palms, then smell his hands. Then he'd tap it and finger it like a blind man. Sometimes he made me close my eyes and, when I'd had a bite, ask me to say which apple."

"You mean d'Arcy Spice or Cox's Orange?"

She laughed. "Oh no, that would have been too easy, like salt and pepper. I mean apples very much alike in shape and flavour. Like – well Cosette Reine and Coseman Reinette. I'm an apple expert. Apples are the only exam I could ever hope to pass."

Then, quite unexpectedly, she asked if she could see my living quarters and we climbed there. "So this is where you spy on us during Sunday services?" she said, poking her head past my baluster and looking down. "What an elevating picture we must make!"

I told her that she'd been safe; I'd only been able to see her hat. "The light straw one," I said. "That's my favourite. Particularly when you stick a rose in the ribbon."

"Stick a rose! Really! Let me tell you, sir, Sara van Fleet isn't any old rose. And it's late in the day to be telling me now. If I'd known, I'd have worn it each Sunday. I don't think Arthur knows what I'm wearing."

Then she turned and went across to the south window. For a while she stood without speaking. Then she said, "So Mr Moon found it after all?"

Oh, why not? I thought. It's going to be published anyway. So I told her what he'd been doing and leaned forward to point out the site of the Anglo-Saxon chapel. She also turned so that her breasts were pressing against me. And, although we both looked outwards across the meadow, she didn't draw away as quite easily she could have done.

I should have lifted an arm and taken her shoulder, turned her face and kissed her. It was that kind of day. It was why she'd come. Then everything would have been different. My life, hers. We would have had to speak and say aloud what both of us knew and then, maybe, turned from the window and lain down together on my makeshift bed. Afterwards, we would have gone away, maybe on the next train. My heart was racing. I was breathless. She leaned on me, waiting. And I did nothing and said nothing.

She drew back and said shakily, "Well, thank you for showing me. I shall have to hurry away; Arthur will be wondering what's become of me. No, please don't come down."

Then she was gone.

I must have stayed alone there for a couple of hours, sitting on the floor, my back to the belfry wall. Once I heard Kathy Ellerbeck calling from below, but I didn't answer and she went off.

Next day, Sunday, she wasn't in church and I couldn't face Moon, chapel, or the Ellerbecks, so I set off across the fields, not following paths, but through gaps and over walls, towards the west. I'd never been that way before. There was warmth and ripeness in the air. Autumn was burning across the Vale, the beeches flaring like torches as the heat mist ebbed away from hedges and spinneys and from flocks grazing along the slopes of the faded fields. Yet, unwilling as I was to acknowledge it, I knew now that this landscape was fixed only momentarily. The marvellous weather was nearing its end.

It was dark when I got back, so late that there were no lights in the village windows. Even so, weary as I was, I knew that I shouldn't sleep so, turning past Moon's darkened tent, I stumbled off down the vicarage's tunnel of a drive. When I came out in the carriage drive-around and stood before the house, the moon had risen above the trees, flooding the scene with light. A bedroom window was open and, for a few minutes, it seemed that Alice was standing there in her nightdress, had caught sight of me and was waving.

But it was only a curtain caught by a gust of the night breeze.

I didn't know what I hoped might happen, nor how long I stayed there, nor have I any recollection of returning to the belfry and to bed. Since, I sometimes have wondered if it was a dream.

*

Next morning I stayed in the belfry, on the boards, propped against one wall, staring at another. Once I heard Charles Moon calling me and, now and then, footsteps (but never hers) below in the building. Then, towards evening, I pulled myself together and thought, Well, usually there's a second chance for most of us; perhaps she's waiting there as I'm waiting here.

Yet, when I reached the carriage drive-around, I found it hard to approach nearer and, had I stopped, might have turned and gone back. Then I was standing on that absurd portico, within a pace of the door itself – and breathless as though I had been running.

How does one know that a house is empty? That house was and I knew it. I knew it even before my knocking was unanswered, even before I stooped to raise the flap of the letter-box to peer into a darkness so concealing that only memory led me back along the stone-flagged corridors, into shuttered rooms, up uncarpeted staircases.

They're not here, I thought. They've gone. And I turned away.

Then I remembered the bell, its mean little knob sagging from a hole bored through a doorpost, its rusting wire disappearing into the darkness and silence. And I pulled at it, hearing at first only a rasping scrape until, far-off, deep inside the empty house, a bell answered: it stirred the stillness for no more than a moment. Yet, high on some wall, it must have still quivered like a live thing.

What came over me? A sort of madness I suppose, because I gripped that knob more firmly and dragged at it again and again so that the bell's sound came hurrying along corridors, round corners, down staircases, echoing and re-echoing, spreading through the dark and empty house like ripples of her laughter. But now I knew that it was laughter calling to me from the past – clearly, playfully, yet poignantly sad. It was the worst moment of my life.

And I dragged at the wire again and again, savagely, despairingly. For how long I cannot say, but when, at last, I turned away and went, I knew that I should never see her again.

Somehow I got through the rest of the day and, during the night, a wind got up, threshing through the ash trees, driving in great gusts at the tower so that, for the only time I lived in that tiny room, the bell above me stirred. It was no more than a thin sound pared from its rim. Half-asleep, I wondered what its significance might be, but in the morning it had become no more than a sound heard in the night.

Then it was one of those marvellously clear days which come after a good blow. The trees had stripped down to their black bones and had heaped leaves in drifts against hedges and walls. Children played amongst them, tossing armfuls into the air, screaming in and out like swimmers at the sea's edge. I saw roofs and walls and gardens hidden from me before. It was astonishing, like looking for the first time at a map of a place one believed one knew well and now finding new holes and corners.

I looked down from the window for a long time; summer and autumn had gone. During the night, the year had crossed into another season. In yards and gardens people were pulling up, burning, trimming, strengthening fences, scraping gutters. They had come out, answering a summons as naturally as the swallows gathering on the telegraph wires and the hedgehogs snuffling into hedge-bottom's rubbish to sleep out the winter. They were doing as their forebears, the men and women on my wall-painting, had done – battening down before winter's onslaught.

That morning I had my first letter. Heaven knows how she had learnt where I was, but it was from Vinny: she wanted me home again. There were other things too but that's what it amounted to – she wanted me back. I had no illusions. She would go off again, would come back again. And I should be there.

When I'd read it, I packed up my gear – everything but my remarkable overcoat. I left it hanging on its nail for Mossop: he'd pointedly admired it more than once and I'd nothing else to give him. Then I went down and had a last look round. The good old Bankdam-Crowther, now reprieved – perhaps this was the moment to put it through its paces and depart in a climacteric roar of smoke and sparks? Then I dawdled down behind the south arcade to second for the last time her grieving husband's Farewell to Laetitia.

"Ah, amantissima et delectissima.
Vale"

And I thought, Perhaps you did well to leave early; it may not have lasted.

Last of all, I gazed beyond the scaffolding to the great painting half hidden in the shadows. Truthfully, I felt nothing much. Certainly no more than a bricklayer may feel as he goes on to a new house. There had been a grey wall and now there were shapes and colours.

So I humped my pack and went out into the yard. Though it was past nine, the grass was soaking with dew and cobwebs drifted, breaking away from bushes and briars. All was as it had been – the fields, the high woods, even the crouching cat. It stared hostilely at me as I lifted the loop of binder-twine to open the gate, meaning to cross the meadow to say cheerio to Moon before going down to the station and the Ellerbecks. Then (and I can't explain it) the numbness went and I knew that, whatever else had befallen me during those few weeks in the country, I had lived with a very great artist, my secret sharer of the long hours I'd laboured in the half-light above the arch. So I turned and climbed the ladder for a last look. And, standing before the great spread of colour, I felt the old tingling excitement and a sureness that the time would come when some stranger would stand there too and understand.

It would be like someone coming to Malvern, bland Malvern, who suddenly is halted by the thought that Edward Elgar walked this road on his way to give music lessons or, looking over to the Clee Hills, reflects that Housman had stood also in that place, regretting his land of lost content. And, at such a time, for a few of us there will always be a tugging at the heart – knowing a precious moment had gone and we not there.

We can ask and ask but we can't have again what once seemed ours for ever – the way things looked, that church alone in the fields, a bed on a belfry floor, a remembered voice, a loved face. They've gone and you can only wait for the pain to pass.

All this happened so long ago. And I never returned, never wrote, never met anyone who might have given me news of Oxgodby. So, in memory, it stays as I left it, a sealed room furnished by the past, airless, still, ink long dry on a put-down pen.

But this was something I knew nothing of as I lifted the loop and set off across the meadow.

Stocken, Presteigne
September, 1978